# TIM HARTWELL
## and the Death of Ages

Aeneas Middleton

TIM HARTWELL and The Death of Ages

Copyright © 2013 by Aeneas Middleton

All Rights Reserved. Under the U.S. Copyright Act of 1976, no part of this publication may be reproduced, distributed, or transmitted in any form or by any means, or stored in a database or retrieval system, without the prior written permission of the publisher.

Royal Middleton publishing
New York, NY
royalmiddletonpublishing@gmail.com

ISBN-13: 978-0615612485
ISBN-10: 0615612482

Library of Congress Control Number:  2012904215

Middleton, Aeneas, 1980-
*Tim Hartwell and The Death of Ages*: by Aeneas Middleton

1st Edition | Series 1
Book Three (Bk. 3)
Copyedited by Ruth Goodman

Printed in the United States of America

Cover and book design by Aeneas Middleton

1  2  3  4  5  6  7  8  9  10  11

TIM HARTWELL and The Death of Ages

# Goddess Venus

MOTHER TO AENEAS OF TROY

3

# TIM HARTWELL series

**Tim Hartwell and The Magical Galon of Wales** (Book One)

**Tim Hartwell and The Brutus of Troy** (Book Two)

**Tim Hartwell and The Death of Ages** (Book Three)

**\*Tim Hartwell and The Wizards of Windsor** (Book Four)

**\*TBA** (Book Five)

**\*TBA** (Book Six)

**\*TBA** (Book Seven)

**\*TBA** (Book Eight)

**\*TBA** (Book Nine)

[\*Coming soon]

# Contents

6      When Twins Are Born

36      Emosiwn Melyn Diamonds

48      When a Fairy Is Born

66      Find Hynwyn Reese

100      Love from Venus

124      Mary's Escape

138      Jealousy from Across

165      When A Kingdom Falls

202      The Bluebells Forest

238      Coat of Arms Castles Death

# When Twins Are Born

**B**ledri and Tomes, the rulers of the House of Cynfor, are standing in front of hundreds of Cynfor dragon gatekeeper soldiers. The new rulers of the House of Cynfor are sitting on their royal thrones inside chamber *Cynforanyth Senate Hall*, which is perpendicular to the Gates of Death. The sound of an old metal ship having its parts ripped away for demolition catches Tomes' attention as gusts of wind fly through the Senate Hall where titan-sized

Cynfor dragons are patiently waiting with their Cynfor coat of arms on their armor and their helmets sparkling in the slight darkness of the Cynforanyth Senate Hall. Fyanicrum and his lionface Jupira are sitting in their royal seats next to Derilyn and his lionface Geulia.

"Hear me, hear me!" Bledri says, pounding his scepter, which has a *Emosiwn Melyn* diamond the size of a grapefruit on top with the Coat of Cynfor engraved midway through the handle. Bledri looks over toward Tomes, eager to inform his men of the news that has come from Stratford.

"We are now in control of the biggest mines in all the Death of Ages!" Bledri shouts as the low-level Gatekeeper dragons stand guard around the chamber, tapping their swords on the ground and making fire sparks. The Gatekeepers continue to tap their large human-size blades on the stone floor as Bledri speaks.

"The power of the *Caves of Siôr* is under our control, effective this very day. Therefore, we will punish any spirit in the Death of Ages that believes they can smuggle our precious Emosiwn Melyn diamonds to their outer regions. As you know, the House of Diablo Arches has been controlling the Caves of Siôr from the beginning of Selwyn's Chancer."

Bledri expresses the anguish his race has been going through over the money, power, and control generated from the Emosiwn Melyn diamonds, for they will keep every single slave as currency given by other Gatekeepers to the House of Cynfor to make a profit in the gladiator games.

"We have new fighters and slaves in the chamber, I see," Bledri says, pointing to many of the fighters who are below them looking up. "Most of you have abandoned your race, even shamed your House names. But not here. You will fight in the games and you will mine our diamonds for an eternity. Nothing more, nothing less."

Bledri continues speaking as Tomes, the lionface head, nudges Bledri about a few things he hasn't pointed out. Bledri shakes his head from left to right and continues to speak on what Tomes foresees.

"As of today, we are expecting two guests who will be arriving very soon. First, a boy wizard descendant of the House of

Hartwell, and second, a young girl, the last descendant of the House of Gwynwell."

The neck of another dragon comes from behind the royal drapes that reach high to the Cynforanyth Senate Hall ceiling behind them. The Cynfor Gatekeeper whispers in Bledri's ear, then in Tomes' ear. Jupira looks on, suspicious of what is being said but unable to make out the Gatekeeper's words.

Bledri slams his scepter on the floor once more, ending the introduction to the Death of Ages meeting. In an instant, Bledri and Tomes follow the Gatekeeper behind the curtains while the remaining low-level Cynfor soldiers start pushing the new spirit slaves toward the freezing-cold dungeons.

Derilyn and Fyanicrum shout at the

top of their lungs toward their low-level command, ordering them to get ready and head toward the Caves of Siôr. Everyone leaves the Senate Hall when the Wyvern twin gargoyles, Alfred and Verlock, uncloak from invisibility, rubbing their hands together with excitement. The Wyvern twins quickly disappear into thin air, whispering to each other.

"They're completely hatstand," Verlock says before they jet toward the stone battlements of the legendary House of Cynfor castle.

On the opposite side of Selwyn's Chancer, Stratford whispers "Tim Hartwell" to himself as Lylock walks into the library of Amelia's Chamber, which is inside Amelia's fortress that's located inside the belly of her titaness Alynn dragon. The personal guards who walked Lylock inside the chamber close the large doors behind him. The father and ruler of the House of Diablo Arches, Lylock is wearing his infamous pink and yellow Emosiwn Melyn diamond coronet, which is sparkling through the room along with the epic chandelier above them. The fortress rumbles for a second, for the Alynn dragon is getting tired in flight as it descends from a patch of cumulonimbus clouds to rest near a hidden section of Foel-goch, a massive mountain in Snowdonia, Wales.

Stratford is sitting in human form, thanks to Amelia's magic. Lylock looks around the ancient library with many books that go back as far as early human and dragon civilization. Stratford continues to look down toward his chess pieces, playing with a few of them with his fingers. He has gotten word that Amelia is going to make a magical spell and birth his first child, and he is overly excited about the magical powers his child might have when born from the bloodline of the House of Hartwell.

Stratford waiting in the library focused. He personally invited Lylock to play a few rounds of chess with him while he waits for Amelia to use her magic, she can make herself go into labor.

Both of them remain quiet as they begin setting up their chess pieces one by one. Each chess piece is made from Emosiwn Melyn diamonds, except for the queens, which Stratford keeps as precious red rubies that remind him of Amelia's favorite stone on Mother Earth. Lylock, with a disturbed look, glances at one of the paintings, since he isn't used to seeing Stratford in human form.

"Are you comfortable with my appearance, Lylock? You seem a bit edgy," Stratford says. "Humans are ugly creatures, I must say. Their bodies are so fragile. You know, our race looks upon that as a weakness."

Lylock thinks about how complex human anatomy is. "Well, if you were human, maybe you wouldn't like your beast appearance either."

Snapping his fingers, Stratford turns Lylock into a handsome middle-aged man, which startles Lylock, making him jump out of his seat and look at his hands. Stratford snaps his fingers once more, making two beautiful blond and brunette archangels appear next to him.

They begin to rub Lylock's shoulders and caress his auburn human hair. Lylock, for a moment, is pleased with his new company but hates his appearance with a passion.

Stratford snaps his fingers, making the women disappear and turning Lylock back into his Diablo Arches beast form.

"That's more like it!" Lylock says, rubbing his jagged hair and looking at himself in a mirror to the left of him.

"Okay, since you're the guest, make your first move," Stratford says.

Lylock stares down at his chess pieces, moving his pawn in a conservative manner to A3. Stratford puts his hand on his chin to think for a moment. He adjusts his thoughts and moves his pawn to B5.

After an hour of playing, the fireplace begins to dim and there are only a few pieces left on the chessboard, with Lylock surprisingly in the lead.

"It looks like you might walk out of here with a sure win," Stratford says firmly. He suddenly thinks about his unborn child as he chooses his next move wisely.

Lylock, in his best interests, abruptly brings up some disturbing news that has been going around the House of Diablo Arches.

"Lord Stratford, I wonder why you have not killed the son of Hartwell, the boy you call Tim Hartwell."

Stratford looks up at him, wondering why Lylock would question his authority, especially at this time.

"Be patient, my friend. For even though the House of Cynfor wants Tim dead after killing Miniver and Cynhafar at World's End, Bledri and Tomes wonder why I am keeping your vicious House alive at all in Selwyn's Chancer. Thanks to me, I understand that wars in the Death of Ages have gotten out of control. Why do you think I made your House second of them all, even though you failed again miserably at Llyn Cwellyn," Stratford says to Lylock about their rational decision making. He always felt the House of Diablo Arches needed to be more organized during war.

"If it wasn't for Brutus of Troy, we would

have captured that little brat," says Lylock, trying to explain his failures.

"I don't want to hear that," Stratford says. "I know you guys can handle the business. But your House failures have now forced me to honor the royal House of Cynfor in full control of your Caves of Siôr.

**"You have done what!!!"**
Lylock screams at the top of his lungs.

"Sit down. Or would you rather me **reverse...** my decision of your House being number two," Stratford says with a callous tone. "I had to give them something down there. Besides, your House has been controlling the trades of Emosiwn Melyn diamonds for ages. If you can do me a small favor, I will return the favor a million times fold." Stratford tries to give Lylock an even better proposition.

"How would you like to be the rulers of the Death of Ages in Selwyn's Chancer forever?" says Stratford, giving a piece of his final plan to his best friend, King Lylock. "I need you to gather your House and start a war for me, a war beyond anything you have ever done for me, my dearest Lylock."

"Tell me, Lord Stratford, for I am eager to know what I must do to control such power," says Lylock, expressing a deep passion to fulfill his duty of finally controlling a god-like power inside Selwyn's Chancer.

Stratford looks directly into the eyes of Lylock, reaching over to Lylock's chess pieces on the board. "I want you to kill a King. Two heads, to be exact," Stratford says as he slides out of his seat, looking over to his enormous book collection. He then looks up toward the second-level walkway with a spiral staircase that goes up to a secret room that no one, except Stratford and Amelia, has been in. This is a secret room that Stratford keeps a spell over, for it can never be opened by anyone except him and his beloved mate.

King Lylock stands quickly to his feet, almost not knowing what to say. He doesn't know exactly what Stratford is talking about.

"I want you to kill every descendant of the House of Cynfor. You will control the depths of Selwyn's Chancer if you succeed. Can you do that for me, Son?" Stratford says with a sparkle in his eyes.

"Lord Stratford, I have been waiting many ages for those words to come from your mouth. You have chosen wisely to believe in the House of Diablo Arches, My Master." Lylock roars with joy as he walks around the room to where Stratford is standing.

"When I call for you, you need to act quickly, and the Death of Ages will be yours. Just remember that," Stratford replies as one of his personal guards interrupts him about Amelia going into labor.

Stratford notices Baron Milwr peeking inside the doorway. Baron quickly stares at the pink and yellow Emosiwn Melyn diamond coronet on the wall near Stratford's head for protection against Baron's voice. Stratford looks back at him with a larger Emosiwn Melyn diamond on his hand, just to show off a bit. He moves his head when Lylock notices the Coat of Hartwell tattooed on Stratford's human wrist. Stratford morphs back into his beast form, keeping a human torso and human arms and legs.

"When you attack the House of Cynfor, you better return Mother Mary to me alive. The wizard's mother.

**Do you hear me?"**

Stratford screams loudly, still thinking about his unborn child on the way. He readjusts and speaks to Lylock, who truly is his best friend, in a more respectful manor.

"Mary must remain alive when you attack the castle to the House of Cynfor. Don't fail me now, Lylock, for your future kingdom will be set with you and Baron Milwr and, of course, all of the House of Diablo Arches." He looks directly into Lylock's eyes.

22

For some reason, he doesn't mind his House failures at this moment. The power of Tim Hartwell has opened more realms inside Selwyn's Chancer. He can feel it.

Stratford gives a few more orders while in the presence of Lylock, but Baron can only think about the Emosiwn Melyn diamonds as precious fruit to his mind.

Stratford waves them off, getting back to the task at hand, running to see Amelia while Baron and Lylock quickly fly like a rocket jet out the stomach of the Alynn dragon, through an opening in the throat, escaping the fire and phlegm inside its mouth. They bank toward the upper region of the cumulous grey clouds above Pembrokeshire Coast National Park. The enormous Alynn dragon soars high above huge cumulus nimbus clouds toward St. Guards, fading into the sky past St. Brides Bay.

Back inside the Alynn dragon, Stratford flies down the royal arched hallways where large drapes have the Coat of Hartwell embroidered on every edge, the four wings and the keyhole centered between them. The red drapes flow throughout the master royal bedroom chamber where Amelia is located. Stratford transforms himself into his human appearance, his eyes glowing slightly as he rushes to hold Amelia's hand.

"My love, is that you?" Amelia whispers toward Stratford. His medium-sized ears can hear every word crystal clear. Amelia takes full control of Stratford's mind without him even knowing while he holds her hand and whispers "I love you." She makes herself fall silently asleep although her body is fully awake and functional.

A white flash magically turns into a magical spirit, which begins to speak to Stratford. It appears to be an obstetrician the way she is dressed.

"She is due any minute now." The woman explains she is Amelia's spirit, Megan Lynelle, a resurrected spirit from her **Alynn-tusk spell**, which allows her to split her spirits in two. Amelia is hesitant to have anyone touch her unborn baby, especially someone who might try to assassinate her firstborn. Amelia's mind silently asleep as her body continues to push the baby out of her womb. Stratford looks on, for he knows this has been her dream for as long as he can remember.

Stratford stands there, almost unfazed by Amelia's second spirit. He holds Amelia's warm hands while he stands by her side, then grips her hands to support her, giving Amelia the assurance of safety while her body pushes in agony.

Eight hours pass and Amelia still hasn't given birth. The stress level skyrockets in Amelia's birthing chamber. Stratford is sweating heavily on the side of his face, for he is patiently awaiting the arrival of his heir to the throne.

Fifteen minutes pass, then Lynelle raises her right hand, signaling that a baby's leg is coming from out of Amelia's womb.

**"It's a boy!"**

Stratford yells loudly while Lynelle, holding a

cloth in one hand, pulls the baby out by the legs.

"He was born feet first," Megan Lynelle says.

Stratford smiles from ear to ear, amazed at the very sight of his son who has brunette hair with a golden lock behind his right ear. Lynelle wipes blood from the boy's skin as she uses magical sterilized scissors to cut the umbilical cord. Lynelle holds the baby directly in front of Amelia's sweaty face for her to see her son, then hands the infant to Stratford to hold. Megan raises her hand once more. Lynelle does the same with her right hand, noticing the top of another baby's head that is beginning to poke out from Amelia's womb.

"There is another!" Lynelle shouts.

Stratford holds his newborn son in his arms as Megan Lynelle speaks to Amelia's body, waking her human spirit. Amelia's spell over Stratford begins to lift. He looks toward her for a quick moment, wondering why Amelia didn't bring out Megan while Tim was in the castle previously. He thinks maybe Lynelle knows something he doesn't but dismisses those thoughts, snapping back into the moment, holding his newborn son while Amelia cries. She has never seen something so angel-like in the dark world they thrive in every day, especially being secluded inside her enormous, but precious, Alynn dragon.

At the same time, Lynelle begins to pull the second baby out and notices it's not a boy. "They are fraternal twins!" says Lynelle, speaking frantically as she looks at the baby girl with blonde hair and eyes the color of a tropical-blue ocean. Megan begins to tend to the baby and does all the necessary things for the second baby to be stable and healthy, for a new heir prince and princess have been born.

A few hours pass and Stratford remains inside the birthing chamber with Amelia, who is totally exhausted. Amelia's second spirit Lynelle tends to the babies while giving the son to Stratford and the girl to Amelia. Lynelle's spirit disappears, which means Amelia's spirit is whole again. Amelia looks so proud to have a daughter as well.

"Twins? What shall we name them, my love?" Amelia's words move through the chamber. Stratford looks down at his son and then his daughter and then back again. He begins to think really hard for a boy's name that sounds strong to reign over his empire through the ages. The large castle sways a bit inside the belly of the Alynn dragon as the dragon begins to wake up near the mountains high above the clouds of Snowdonia in northwest Wales.

"We shall call our beloved new prince **Cayne (Welsh: Spear)**. He will be my new heir. We will also make a statue of them both at the Carantoc Gladiator Arena in the Death of Ages. I will then make sure everyone knows he will rule at the right age," Stratford says with utmost confidence, for he knows his son will have his very own magical powers that will reveal themselves soon enough.

Amelia looks at Stratford to continue,

for he knows his daughter must have a name just as honorable. So he names the Princess of Selwyn's Chancer after his dear love, Amelia.

"She will be called **Amelia II**. She will be an equal ruler beside Cayne until he comes of age to rule the royal throne of Selwyn's Chancer. Our little princess will control all dragons and ice when Cayne becomes King. She will have some control. It could be decent for the both of them in the long run. They both will be a force to be reckoned with."

Stratford can feel the endless knowledge of the parallel world within Selwyn's Chancer looking at them. Stratford glances at Amelia's beautiful eyes; love has sprouted from their hearts. Stratford always knew he needed the presence of knowledge, and the only way to be a true King is to have a true Queen.

**"Open Your Heart, Trust Your Heart,"** Stratford whispers to himself, reciting one of many House of Hartwell family quotes.

Stratford takes both children so Amelia can sleep. Her twin spirit Lynelle illuminates once more to take care of the twin babies. Stratford has a clear mind and peace traveling through his heart for his new children and beautiful Queen. He walks out of the bedroom chamber, all the way outside to the gates of Amelia's Chamber to the castle.

Stratford walks toward the heart of Amelia's Alynn dragon, which is beneath a glass floor below his feet. The dragon's heart is thumping loudly. Stratford just stands there with his pink and canary-yellow Emosiwn Melyn diamond coronet around his head, his enormous ring shining in peace. At this moment, Stratford is thirsty for all of the hidden power in the parallel world of Selwyn's Chancer that has created itself, thanks to Tim's mother giving him the 1st Galon key. He thinks about the magical possibilities that will occur.

Stratford looks down at the Alynn's dragon heart smothered in lava, beating like a drum. Some of the lava splashes against the other side of the glass below his feet. Stratford smiles, knowing he has seized the moment of future power like he did before trapping the House of Cynfor in the Death of Ages forever.

## Chapter 1: When Twins Are Born

Stratford drinks some wine in an oval glass as he continues to stare at the beauty of the dragon heart, beating with a deep tone, wondering if his children will have twin-telepathy. He looks up at the Diablo Arches on top of the castle with their flat heads and black bodies, guarding the purple-toned crystal castle.

The huge panther, Sylkin, catches Stratford's eye and tries to make an impression for a quick snack. Sylkin jumps up with excitement, forgetting the large chain connected to the collar around his neck, which brings his body slamming back down to the rocky ground. Stratford points on the side of Sylkin, magically making a Tyrannosaurus rex appear right in front of Sylkin. In a flash, Sylkin goes in for the kill at lightning speed, leaping toward the Tyrannosaurus that roars back unafraid. With a quick attack, Sylkin's razor-sharp teeth sink into the neck of the Tyrannosaurus and snap off its neck and head.

As twilight passes outside North Wales, Stratford begins to think about a genius idea: using Sylkin to help, along with the House of Diablo Arches, when they invade the House of Cynfor.

Emosiwn Melyn Diamonds

Deep inside the raging world of the Death of Ages lies the Caves of Siôr, resting below another patch of clouds drifting across the earth's troposphere. Below the clouds are large waterfalls in the middle of the desert outskirts. At this very moment, the House of Cynfor, for the first time in the Death of Ages, has control of the precious diamonds that shine like no other diamonds in the universe. Each diamond keeps the House of Cynfor very happy about the control of the Caves of Siôr.

Bledri and Tomes' egos are through the roof as they arrive outside the Caves of Siôr with dragon Fyanicrum, and his lion-face head Jupira. Accompanying them are their partners, who are third to the throne, the Cynfor dragon named Derilyn and his lionface head Guelia. Standing behind them all are their royal personal guards, including a few Gatekeepers from the Gates of Death. All of them are covered in armor with capes dangling from their backs. The royal House of Cynfor's coat of arms is on all of their armor, weaponry, and apparel.

Somehow, Tomes has gotten excited from his *born-drunken slumber*. Their father wanted to make Derilyn and Geulia second in line, but for politics over the Senate, Miniver and Cynhafar were named third in line to the throne.

Tomes, at this very moment, feels the triumphs of power and magically straightens his neck, looking through the fifth-level window to see a mountainous cave interior with a path that stretches into darkness. Tomes' lionface head seems more intelligent at this moment.

"How could this be?" Bledri whispers to himself, watching his brother, Tomes, look around, sniffing the air for any scent of a trap by the Diablo Arches. He knows a few of them can never be trusted because of their strong ties with Stratford. Bledri and Tomes both understand that Lylock and

Baron Milwr and their House of Diablo Arches have been in control of the caves prior to their arrival in Selwyn's Chancer.

As everyone continues to look around the fifth-level chamber, Fyanicrum and Jupira notice a letter nailed to a wooden stake in the ground toward the lower exitway chamber. The letter, which has a candle-wax seal, sways from side to side as a gust of wind creeps its way up from the lower chambers.

"This seal is from Nessa and Elle Milwr, the daughters of Lylock and sisters to brother Baron Milwr," Fyanicrum says.

"Nessa was almost killed by the voice of her own brother, as her Emosiwn Melyn necklace had fallen off a cliff where they were arguing one night, I have heard,"

Bledri says to Fyanicrum.

"If it wasn't for Lylock, Nessa would be dead. I was shocked to hear Lylock had enough time to wrap a spare coronet of Emosiwn Melyn diamonds around her head to save her, for her eardrums are still severely damaged." Tomes speaks unexpectedly, for none of the other Cynfor lionface heads can speak.

"So that is why their father, Lylock, has given Nessa and Elle the power of being speakers of the House and over business throughout the Caves of Siôr. Lylock and Baron don't know how to write words after all," Fyanicrum says with laughter.

"But they can still read!" Bledri says with a firm voice as he waves his arm for Fyanicrum and Jupira to snap back into formation to read the letter out loud to their rulers. Fyanicrum and Jupira pull the letter off the wooden stake as they walk in formation. Fyanicrum reads the letter out loud.

"The House of Cynfor, for this day forth, will inherit leadership of the Caves of Siôr. All of the slaves or beasts who mine in the Caves of Siôr are locked up in their cells, occupying 2nd and 3rd low-level chambers. All monitoring, logs, and security-line sequencing are left inside the master guarding chamber on the 4th-level chamber, which controls most of the complex. Watch your back, for the prisoners have become restless as you transport more of them into the cells. We are sure your House will do fine in this manner. Sincerely,

The House of Diablo Arches."

Another patch of Gatekeepers is sent from the castle to Bledri and Tomes so they can restore order in the Caves of Siôr to their liking. In some way, Bledri and Tomes are still wondering why Stratford would freely give away anything, especially control of the pinnacle of wealth in Selwyn's Chancer. Both Bledri and Tomes shrug off the idea, as Stratford predicted to perfection that their instinct race would. Genius.

The House of Cynfor make all the necessary **Trancynformation** inside the Caves of Siôr, including schedules for feeding all the spirit slaves, while Bledri and Tomes walk through the 2nd- and 3rd-level chambers, looking at some of the slaves in their cells, for they haven't been given access inside the Gates of Death. Most of them were caught by the House of Diablo Arches while others made deals with the House of Scorpus, only to find themselves in the Death of Ages, caught by the Vonixra beasts and later sold to the House of Diablo Arches for Emosiwn Melyn diamonds.

Bledri and Tomes start mapping out the remaining cave interior, which is the size of the *Ogof Ffynnon Ddu* caves in South Wales. They head back up to the 4th-level chamber, walking out onto the balcony that oversees the 2nd- and 3rd-level chambers that have more than three hundred cells. Bledri grips the safety pipe along the balcony and begins to address all the slaves about their new twenty-three-hour work schedules, giving them one hour for leisure time so they can still fight each other in the annual *Carantoc Gladiator Games,* which are coming up tomorrow in the early afternoon.

A few hours pass. A small Cynfor runner goes by. He looks like a lizard with a branded Cynfor coat of arms on his back. The runner informs his rulers of possible intruders within their castle grounds.

"I told you we should have stayed back at the castle and come here tomorrow, but no. You had to see this place today. I knew I should have listened to my intuition," said Bledri, blaming Tomes for them leaving so soon without capturing Tim's mother, Mary, before the arrival of Tim Hartwell and Ceri Gwynwell.

Bledri orders Fyanicrum and Guelia to

44

stand guard at the Caves of Siôr and keep them informed of the progress of mining throughout the caves, for they have some very important business to take care of, including the treatment for the Carantoc Gladiator Games.

Bledri and Tomes wrap things up and head back to their castle to capture their intruders, for they know who they are, except for the rest of the royal House of Cynfor.

"Bledri and Tomes have already broken a few rules by not including the Senate Hall on situations involving the House," Verlock says to his brother, Alfred, the Wyvern gargoyles who are spying on them for Stratford. The brothers magically appear with their eyes illuminating, but they remain invisible, hiding inside the chamber.

As Bledri and Tomes head back to Cynfor castle, Fyanicrum and Jupira walk back up to the 5th level, looking at all the Emosiwn Melyn diamonds in the cave once more. Derilyn and Guelia pull the levers for all the slaves to get working and start mining more diamonds for them.

At this very moment, tension between the slaves and the House of Cynfor has risen, for the slaves really understand even more now. This has to be the worst thing to happen to them in ages, even under the leadership of the House of Diablo Arches.

Fyanicrum looks on as the royal Cynfor dragon personal guards stand guard in their places. The slaves, holding torches, form lines leading down into the pits of the caves. The light from their torches begins to illuminate farther down the cave from the royal observation side-chamber.

"The fire of their torches is burning fiercely," Fyanicrum says to Jupira.

"I hope their inner fire can last for all time, for now the House of Cynfor will grip the power for our beloved Bledri and Tomes forever in the Death of Ages, for we will put our lives on the line for such a treasure," agrees Jupira, who nods and continues to look down at history in the making.

# When A Fairy Is Born

On the other side of the castle to the House of Cynfor, Tim is watching the Gates of Death open slowly as the T-Rex dinosaur skull slides up. The light behind the gates begins to blind Tim and Ceri. In a flash, they open their eyes to see no one there, just a long path directly in front of them with trees stretching from left to right as far as they can see.

Tim and Ceri look farther down the

48

path ahead of them, noticing a castle far off in the distance. Tim becomes very suspicious, for he doesn't see the Gatekeepers or Cynfor dragons anywhere.

"How could they disappear so quickly?" Ceri says. "They must be using some type of magic to transport themselves to different parts of the Death of Ages."

The Gates of Death shut with a loud bang. Suddenly, Ceri grabs her chest and begins to feel the transformation of her becoming the watcher of the Last Fairy Maze Forest. With hesitation and to slow the process, she quickly pulls out the canister that Darron, one of the rulers from the House of Scorpus, had given her. Ceri quickly pulls out the cork and drinks some of the liquid. She begins coughing hard because of the taste of the liquid exstraction, which is made from poisonous leaves that grow outside the castle of the hidden House of Scorpus in North Wales.

"This is some of the most unpleasant stuff I've ever drunk in my life," Ceri says. She tucks the canister back in her cloak.

Ceri and Tim are still sitting on Jupiter's magical horses, waiting for their next command.

"Good thing they gave it to you, for if it wasn't for Brutus of Troy, we would both be trapped in the upper-region world of Selwyn's Chancer in Snowdon," said Tim.

In a flash, Ceri begins screaming, for the liquid Darron gave her isn't working correctly. Instead, it is speeding up the process of her fairy watcher transformation.

"How, how could they do this to me? They have betrayed us!" Ceri says, screaming as her body slowly begins illuminating. She starts to fade away as her body falls off the horse onto the ground. Tim quickly jumps off his horse to help her but notices that her body has faded away into the ground. He looks up at Jupiter's horse that Ceri was sitting on, noticing that both of the horses have merged into one horse, for the power of Jupiter must know exactly what is going on.

Tim screams with revenge as he looks at the ground, picking up Ceri's cloak. Her signet ring is hovering slightly above the ground, along with her necklace that has a charm with the Gwynwell coat of arms engraved on it.

Crows begin to fly from the treetops to other parts of the forest. Tim, not sure what to do, screams out

**"CERI!!!"**

Tim is breathing erratically, feeling the betrayal once more. He should have known the House of Scorpus was not to be trusted. Tim builds rage in his heart as he thinks about meeting the rulers of the House of Scorpus, Darron and Darryn, and paying them back for what they have done.

Tim looks up and notices the sky

changing from orange to blue. The wind begins to pick up, and the young wizard jumps back on his horse, not sure where to go next. Without warning, Tim hears someone laughing, the sound echoing to the skies. The voice is very familiar. It's the voice of Ceri, who sounds sinister, for she has become the watcher of the Last Fairy Maze Forest after all. The voice begins to speak from inside the forest directly ahead. Tim puts all of Ceri's belongings into a sack on the side of the horse, then immediately rides down the path to where it is split down the middle by a huge tree. There is a wooden Wales coat of arms nailed to the tree with a young girl's face poking through the center of a keyhole on the shield. Only the nose and mouth are exposed.

Tim walks his horse over to the tree and jumps off his horse. He takes the Shield of Aeneas off the side of the horse for protection and walks over to this mysterious

52

female coat of arms object.

"What are you?" Tim says as he rubs his left hand on the side of the shield. Out of nowhere, the girl's face begins to speak.

**"STAND BACK."**

The girl's voice shatters the air with a smooth but rough tone.

"Ceri, is that you?" Tim asks the fairy watcher, who doesn't have eyes.

"Ceri is no more, she is gone forever. You will never escape my forest, young wizard. You will be trapped here for the rest of your miserable life," the voice of Ceri as the fairy watcher replies with a rude tone. Her spirit is controlled by the magical poison from the Gwenwyna.

"Ceri, it's me, Tim. Don't you recognize my voice?" he says with a respectable tone, hoping she will understand.

"Why are you asking questions to answers you already know? Choose your destiny, left or right, dear boy," Ceri says, giving Tim his options of travel through the forest.

"Where can I find Hynwyn Reese, for I know he can help you," Tim says.

"Hahahaha, the mighty barbarian. He should be fighting in the Carantoc Gladiator Games very soon. He can't help you now," she replies, then goes dormant, not saying another word.

Tim's eyes look more determined than ever. He looks left then looks right, noticing both paths seem too similar. He is not sure which way to go. Before he chooses, Tim hears two voices he knows very well. The twin Wyvern gargoyles, Alfred and Verlock, appear behind him.

"Look what she has gotten herself into now, for she was the last bloodline to the House of Gwynwell," Alfred says.

Tim, out of rage, picks Alfred up and slams his back up against a tree, demanding answers.

"I told you he was completely hatstand," Verlock says as the power of the magical Galon begins to make him more enraged.

"We, we can't help you save her. Only Hynwyn Reese knows how to transform her back," says Alfred. "We can tell you which way to go, but that will be all for now. Stratford for sure has his eyes on us all at this very moment. Don't you know Amelia has given birth to a girl and boy, fraternal twins? They will have some of the power of the Galon themselves, for now you know your mother, Mary, should have never given you the Galon back in Tenby."

Tim, holding Alfred by the neck, lets him go. Alfred slides to the ground. Tim lets the Shield of Aeneas slide off his right arm onto the ground next to him. Jupiter's horse snorts as soon as he does, knowing he is losing some of his confidence and needs to shape up.

"Don't give up now, young wizard, for you have a long journey ahead of you, especially since you gave away Adamanthea's rope. You should have never traded it with Emperor Claudius," Alfred says.

"Don't order me around!" Tim screams back at them. Some of the birds chirp in the background, distracting them for a second. Verlock and Alfred look at each other, remembering to keep their promise to help Tim no matter what, even if it gets them killed. In their hearts they are tired of being slaves to Stratford Hartwell.

"Okay, fine. You must go left. This way will lead you to the castle, but you must remember, there will be a storm ahead but you will survive, trust me. Going right will have you lost forever, even though it leads to the Gates of Horn, but not the right way, if you can understand," says Alfred, twisting up his words a bit.

56

The fairy voice begins to speak, for she won't accept anyone tampering with her knowledge of the forest. In mere seconds, tree vines fly toward Verlock and Alfred, grabbing them both, pulling them deep into the forest as they scream for their lives, but for their sakes, they are able to disappear into thin air before the vines crush their bodies like toothpicks.

"Holy Tenby," Tim says, noticing the forest is very alive indeed.

"Listen to them if you must, but you will never escape my realm," Ceri says, trying to discourage Tim from going down the right path. Tim, trusting his twin Wyverns, gathers his things, jumps back on Jupiter's horse, and rides down the left path as fast as he can. Electricity sparks on the ground as the horse runs faster and faster down the path to the back entrance to the castle of the House of Cynfor.

As Tim continues to ride, he notices

more and more wooden coats of arms repeating themselves, with Ceri's face appearing on one tree after another. She is blind but can hear every movement of the horse riding through the forest. Tim, not giving in, continues to ride faster and faster. The sky turns from blue to orange once more, with noctilucent and cirrus spissatus undulatus clouds starting to appear above him far ahead.

"This must be the storm Verlock and Alfred were talking about," Tim says.

Ceri as the fairy watcher begins to laugh louder and louder until Tim approaches part of the forest path that has mist blocking his sight as he rides closer. Tim pulls on the reins for his horse to halt, the dark mist directly in front of him, almost as if the clouds were lowered to the ground on purpose. Tim, not sure what will be waiting for him down this misty path, hears another voice that he for sure will never forget.

"You must continue to believe, Tim, for fear is only an illusion," Goddess Diana says. She appears to the side of him as a mere glow, for day becomes night in seconds. The forest is completely dark, which is going to make it harder for him to travel within the Last Fairy Maze Forest. Another female made of light appears next to Goddess Diana and begins to speak.

"Hello, Tim. I am Goddess Venus, mother of Aeneas from Troy. I am here to give you a bit of knowledge, thanks to Diana informing me of the situation you have been forced into."

Venus and Diana are as tall as some of the trees. They glance down at Tim, their bodies illuminating the ground around him.

"Use the Shield of Aeneas to guide you through the storm. It will help you in many ways as it did Aeneas when he needed it most in Latium," Venus says.

Tim, not really sure what to say, utters

a few words to find out exactly what he must do next. "Tell me what I have to do, Venus. And thank you, Diana. I never expected to see you again." When a Galon key appears around his neck, it's the 7th Galon, the guiding voice of Eleanor Hartwell, who begins to speak.

"Tim, you have the power of the Galon. Use it well. Listen to them both, for they can help you. Besides, I am not sure what fate Ceri will have. You might not be able to save her, but you must escape the Death of Ages with the Book of Hartwell. That is of the utmost importance right now."

Venus looks toward Diana and both of them agree with Eleanor. Venus begins to speak, informing Tim about the magic the Shield of Aeneas has to offer him as he continues his journey to fulfill his magical destiny.

"First, young wizard, I would like to inform you that if and when you escape from the Death of Ages, you will have to return the Shield of Aeneas to its proper owner, for Claudius has concealed the shield for generations without our knowledge. It must be taken away to a safe place, for it must never be in the hands of evil in Tartarus or Selwyn's Chancer. Do you understand me, young wizard?"

Tim replies with a simple nod and bows to the goddess of love and beauty.

"Hold the Shield of Aeneas in front of you. Look at its natural, beautiful, golden color. Feel the engravings, note the triple triumph of Augustus below its center. Nothing can penetrate the shield, for it has been forged by Vulcan under my consent for my son Aeneas. Now you will hold this power in your hands and remember the truth from it. That is the only way for the true magical ability to shine along with the power of your magical Galon ability," says Venus, unfolding more of the truth about the shield.

Tim, eager to ask more questions, cuts her off but not intentionally. He glances over to Diana with her arms crossed, wondering what exactly he will say next.

"Oh, dear Venus, please tell me why Virgil had Aeneas go through the Gates of Ivory instead of the Gates of Horn, for that has been a mystery since the days of Virgil." Tim speaks politely, for he hopes he isn't being rude for wanting to know one of the biggest mysteries in mankind's history.

Venus curls her lip, surprised to hear such wise questions coming from a young boy from the House of Hartwell.

"I will answer this one question and that is all, for you must be on your way," Venus says quickly. "Virgil was correct indeed. Aeneas' spirit was one of the very few to do so. It was based only on the time Aeneas traveled through the Ivory Gate. Aeneas happened to be born in a leap year, which allowed him to be able to travel through the Gates of Ivory, for the dreams he would see would be his future, not lies. Don't forget, Aeneas was alive when he traveled through the underworld. For this was the reason he could have images that would rise in his dreams for him to remember when he was reborn, for all souls are cleansed of their sins and memory. Aeneas would be reborn and his dreams would be the map that would guide him to Latium and his destiny. This is all I will reveal for now."

Venus smiles at Diana. "Now, back to the Shield of Aeneas. If you look at it now, you will see it has a map of the Death of Ages on it. Look. Don't you see?" says Venus, pointing toward the shield engravings that magically turned into a map of the Death of Ages.

"Look now, young wizard, for we must go. You must travel your life as you see fit. *Arma virumque cano*," Venus says to Tim in Latin. "You are the chosen one, my dear boy. You will turn Tenby into one of the greatest cities in the future, as Aeneas did for Rome.

"Oh, and by the way, we see Jupiter's horse has helped you out tremendously," Venus says before Goddess Diana twist up the wind around them and creates a medium-sized tornado, which makes them vanish swiftly into thin air. Tim looks left and right toward the trees. He notices Ceri's face on a tree behind him, watching his every move in the Last Fairy Maze Forest. Parts of Ceri's face are made with small leaves from the forest. She smiles at him, as if she knows something he doesn't.

Tim, unafraid, looks down at the Shield of Aeneas before he slaps the reins on the side of Jupiter's horse, riding off into the mist on the path toward the castle of the House of Cynfor.

"Oh, Ceri, I will save you. I will find

Hynwyn Reese to bring you back by my side. I must save you," Tim says to himself, wondering if he can really save Ceri after all. Tim also ponders why Venus didn't mention the Book of Hartwell but shrugs off the notion, feeling the signs racing through the clouds of mist, praying he will get to the castle in time.

Night is approaching the Death of Ages. The forest is filled with all types of mythical beasts, poisonous creatures, and lost spirits waiting to find any new prey inside the vast lands of the Last Fairy Maze Forest.

Night recedes from the daylight of blue and orange hues. The earth is quiet and the air seems a bit more thin the closer Tim gets to the castle of Bledri and Tomes. He notices the cloud of mist opening ahead of him and altocumulus lenticularis cloud formations above him, even as dawn breaks. Thanks to the 5th Galon, the *Firewyn spell* illuminates a light-blue-colored flame around his arms, lighting up the land around him.

Tim continues riding Jupiter's horse

down the Last Fairy Maze Forest path, finally reaching the back of the castle of the House of Cynfor. He notices the fairy watcher's coat of arms facing his direction on the last tree. Tim looks at the height of the battlements and the length that stretches as far as the horizon, like the previous Gates of Death when he first arrived with Ceri in the legendary Death of Ages.

Tim, more determined than ever, looks up then right, noticing he is located at the west Gates of Death, which don't have a large Tyrannosaurus skull mounted on the front of the titan-sized wooden suicide gate doors directly in front of him. There is a large steel Cynfor coat of arms hammered onto the gates. White smoke is drifting from underneath the gate doors, which catches

Tim's attention. There are a few skeletons on both sides of the western Gates of Death. Each skeleton has one of its arms chained to the wall of the battlements as if people were placed there to be killed by the Cynforian dragons.

Loud roars and earthquake-like thumps on the ground from an unidentified dragon are coming from the misty path behind Tim. Ceri's fairy watcher voice comes at him from the right.

"Are you prepared to die? It's coming for you. There is no escaping the Last Fairy Maze Forest, for I am the watcher. You will die where you stand, young wizard." Ceri's voice sounds scratchy from the magic that has transformed her. She has complete control of the mysterious forest.

The roars behind Tim continue to get louder. He looks back, not seeing a thing through the thick mist down the path, when two unexpected guests appear, perched on top of the Gates of Death, looking down at Tim from high above.

"Use the power that Brutus of Troy has taught you, Tim, for these doors can only be opened by a House of Cynfor or a House of Gwynwell blood descendant. Once you are small enough, you should be able to walk underneath the west Gates of Death," Alfred and Verlock, the twin Wyverns, shout down at him.

A quick snap of Tim's fingers makes Tim, his belongings, and Jupiter's horse shrink to microscopic size right next to the west Gates of Death. The leaves and dirt from the ground seem larger than life. Pieces of dirt are the size of his apartment building back in Tenby, Pembrokeshire.

Tim's ears pick up the roaring, but this time it sounds like a titan, the sound almost hurting his eardrums because of the huge power of the unknown dragon stomping in his direction. The fairy watcher screams for she does not know where Tim has gone. She wonders how he could disappear so quickly without her knowledge.

"Where are you? Where have you gone in my realm," the fairy watcher says.

On Jupiter's horse, Tim rides faster than lightning underneath the Gates of Death. At his microscopic size, it takes him a few minutes to go completely underneath the gate doors. A few miniscule Cynforian bugs that were living underneath the gates notice Tim traveling to the other side. Looking like the perfect meal, they get into attack position from the bottom of the gates, which seem as high as St. Paul's Cathedral in London.

Tim, with quick reaction, shoots out his light-blue flame from his *Firewyn spell* toward six bugs that are bounding toward his location. The fire flame scorches the Cynforian bugs one by one, burning them as they fall down like hot rocks shooting out of an erupting volcano. Their bug legs pop off and their bodies explode into a million burnt pieces of exoskeleton shards. The eyes of Jupiter's horse turn into electrical currents and shoot out lightning, electrocuting more bugs that are trying to sneak attack. Tim looks down at the horse's eyes, surprised that Jupiter has given him some of his magical, god-like power.

As they safely ride underneath the west Gates of Death to the other side, Tim snaps his fingers, turning him and his horse back to normal size. A loud sound shocks them both.

**BANG!**

"What was that?" Tim screams as he grabs the reins. The mysterious dragon beast had slammed its body against the opposite side of the Gates of Death. When Tim turns around, he notices he's standing between the battlements and the lower bailey to the dungeon of Bledri and Tomes.

"Holy Tenby," Tim says to himself, using the words of his best friend, Owen, from his Greenhill School back in Tenby. As the beast smacks the gates from the other side once more, Tim turns around, looking up at the back end of the castle where the entrance of the dungeon leads down into the dungeon cells.

"This must be where all the spirits are locked up. Hynwyn Reese must be here. I have to save Ceri," Tim says to himself, noticing there aren't any Gatekeepers guarding the western Gates of Death.

He notices different Cynfor mid-level dragons patrolling the top of the castle, unaware that Tim has infiltrated the grounds into the lower bailey. The Gatekeepers look down as they hear the sound of the gates being smashed into by the mysterious dragon on the other side.

Tim, quick to think, races toward the walls outside the castle to hide from the Cynfor dragons above him before they notice his intrusion. Sitting on top of Jupiter's horse, Tim remains still with his face toward the stone entrance to the dungeon on his left-hand side leading down into the main entranceway where more Cynfor Gatekeepers are guarding inside.

The House of Cynfor hasn't had an intruder on their grounds since the legendary war between the House of Scorpus, before Darron and Darryn gave up Hynwyn Reese to the House of Cynfor as an offering of peace between the two Houses so they could remain at peace with each other for the time being. Both Houses agreed not to commit any type of viral act of war or high treason against the House of Cynfor.

The twin Wyvern gargoyles, Alfred and Verlock, appear on top of the battlements with their legs draped over the lower bailey. They look down at Tim inside the dungeon that houses all the dead spirits known in Selwyn's Chancer and some from Tartarus. The dungeon, by myth, is impossible for any locked-up spirit to escape.

Some of the slaves have worked their twenty-three hours of the day, and Tim just happens to be going in when they have one hour of leisure time away from working in the Caves of Siôr. The vicious prisoners inside are slaves who compete at the Carantoc Gladiator Games where a raffle is held and a certain number of gladiators are picked to fight against each other until death.

"He's completely hatstand for going in there alone. Is he really going to try and save Hynwyn Reese? I wonder what the House of Scorpus will have to say about that," Verlock says to Alfred.

"I can tell you this, my brother. If he escapes, that will open Pandora's box, and many of the spirits there will believe they can escape as well. I wish him luck, for it is pretty brave of him to try to save Ceri, for she is the last bloodline to the House of Gwynwell. Do you think he can do it, escape the Death of Ages?" Alfred asks Verlock as they continue to look at Tim who gathers his things off Jupiter's horse and walks down the steps of the humongous entrance into the deadly dungeon.

Alfred's eyes cue in on Tim holding

the Shield of Aeneas as Tim uses his power of the 4th Galon to walk through the locked wooden door, which has metal brackets that are unbreakable. Only the strength of Cynfor Dragon Gatekeepers with their oversized shoulders can open the locking system to bring in or let out slaves for the gladiator games or for mining Emosiwn Melyn diamonds.

Verlock looks up and notices the titan Cynfor dragons patrolling on top of the large **Cynforian Keep Station** with their bow and arrows that can kill any titan. The arrows are as thick as tree trunks found in Snowdonia National Park.

"Look at the size of those things!" Verlock says to Alfred before they disappear into the night. Jupiter's horse shrinks to a microscopic size on its own to avoid being captured at it awaits Tim's return from the dungeon. Before the Wyverns disappear Alfred says, "Let's pray for them."

"If only he didn't trade Adamanthea's rope he would of escaped the Death of Ages by morning. Oh, well. It looks like his journey will be harder than we planned," Alfred says.

"Planned? Hogwash!" Verlock whispers. "There should have never been a boy descendant to carry the Galon. What if he didn't ..."

Verlock cuts himself short as they notice some visitors entering the lower bailey from the main bailey. The top Cynforian members of the Cynfor Senate Hall, Ceiro-Eira the dragon head, and Valmai, his lionface head, arrive to check on the living conditions of the prisoners, just in case they need to be disciplined for killing other prisoners during the leisure time during their lunch break in the lower bailey. Ceiro-Eira and Valmai's main objective for this very day is to maintain the prisoners' endurance and health, keeping their muscles toned for mining or for fighting in the gladiator games.

"How many pounds do you think our House will make our majesties when the games begin?" Ceiro-Eira says, his red spiky Mohawk leading all the way down to the end of their tail. Valmai nods his head. As a lionface, he has only learned to speak a few words. He never can pronounce them anyway, so Valmai nods for Ceiro-Eira, letting him know he agrees with his dragon-head part of their rugged-looking body.

"The entire House of Cynfor has complete control of the Caves of Siôr. I am so excited for the Senate Hall; I can see fortunes in the near future. It is long overdue that the House of Diablo Arches has controlled the precious Emosiwn Melyn diamonds," Ceiro-Eira says as they continue to walk slowly toward the entrance of the dungeon.

Ceiro-Eira barks a distinct sound, which alerts the Cynfor dragons at the **Cynforian Keep Station** to open the doors for them to enter. Bledri and Tomes moved the lock switch to open the dungeon doors into the **Cynforian Keep Station** for more protection when they became rulers of the House of Cynfor.

Somewhere in the lower levels of the dungeon, Tim Hartwell is searching for Hynwyn Reese, unaware that he could be caught at any moment and locked in the dungeon of Bledri and Tomes for an eternity.

Tim walks down a narrow path that leads to the second lower level of the dungeon. There is only one way down to the third level, which is marked on the Shield of Aeneas. The engravings on the shield have completely changed due to the power of the Galon.

Tim looks down at the shield, which has a map of the entire dungeon. There is a path that connects the main chamber all the way back to the lower gates to transfer more prisoners underground instead of above ground. Tim hears some voices coming his way. He dashes over to a shadow-hidden pocket as he watches Ceiro-Eira walk directly past him into the **Snowyn Chamber** that keeps ice, which melts and creates a cool ventilation area throughout the castle, including the drinking water system. Ceiro-Eira points toward the ice while Valmai points to a large map on the ceiling showing the locations of the Snowyn Mountains not too far from their location. This is the only place in the Death of Ages that naturally makes ice for the entire House of Cynfor.

"The ice needs to be restocked immediately," Ceiro-Eira says to some of the low-level Cynfor dungeon guards. The guards move in formation to head out to the entranceway of the dungeon that has a long and wide carriage that carries the large slabs of ice back to the castle.

**"Halt!!!"**

Ceiro-Eira says, looking toward his lion-face head Valmai.

"Do you smell that?" Valmai says.

Ceiro-Eira opens his nostrils wide. "I think, I think, I smell living human tissue," he says to Valmai as Fyanicrum and Jupira, third in line to throne, arrive to see Ceiro-Eira.

"You smell what?" Fyanicrum says loudly toward them with suspicion.

"It's nothing, Your Majesty," Ceiro-Eira says, keeping a tight lip, for the last thing they want is for Fyanicrum and Jupira to think they aren't doing their job of watching every metre of the dungeon.

Fyanicrum barks toward the rest of the Cynfor dragons to disperse from the *Snowyn Chamber* and head toward the main building, which is attached to the *Carantoc Gladiator Colosseum*.

"You will be able to finish your work later. It's time to watch the games," says Fyanicrum, reassuring Ceiro-Eira and Valmai that there is nothing to worry about. The entire group leaves the Snowyn Chamber and goes into another hall that leads to another entrance to the dungeon.

Tim Hartwell, unnoticed, is almost frozen to death from the cold temperatures. Tim yells out **"FIREWYN"** to warm his arms with his light-blue flame. The young wizard walks down some of the cold aisles to see if one of the prisoners is Hynwyn Reese. Tim has never seen a picture of the magical barbarian and original ruler of the House of Scorpus.

"Hynwyn Reese, Hynwyn Reese," Tim Hartwell whispers, using the light-blue flame from the *Firewyn spell* of the 5th Galon to brighten the hallways.

"Shh, keep it down, will you, little twerp. You're going to get us all killed," says a raspy voice coming from one of the dark cells. Most of the other prisoners are lying silently in their cells, staying obedient.

Tim slowly walks over to the dark cell, trying to get a better look at who has the courage to speak.

"Keep it quiet," the voice says once more. Tim looks into the left-hand corner of the cell and sees a shadowy figure with long arms and short legs. His name is Caledfryn, and he is an old, hard-nosed Cynfor dragon with only one head. His lionface-head Dazeryn was chopped off for high treason for stealing large amounts of Emosiwn Melyn diamonds and selling them back to the House of Scorpus while keeping all of the profit for himself.

Caledfryn still has the large, thick scar on the side of his neck where the neck of Dazeryn's lionface head used to be. Caledfryn's eyes have remained bloodshot ever since he was punished. The old Cynfor dragon looks down at Tim, who is outside his cell. One claw holds on to the frozen prison bars.

"What is a living soul doing in the dungeon of Bledri and Tomes? How are you even breathing down here?" Caledfryn asks. But before Tim can answer, Caledfryn asks another serious question, for he notices the House of Hartwell coat of arms on Tim's shirt.

"You are the boy descendant of the Galon, you are the one. What the heck are you doing here? What the heck are you doing here?" Caledfryn repeats himself loudly while Tim raises his hand in a gesture for him to keep it down before he alarms one of the Gatekeeper guards.

"I am looking for Hynwyn Reese. Tell me where he is in this dreadful place," Tim says, holding the Shield of Aeneas with ease, for it is as light as a feather for him to carry it long distances.

"Hynwyn, you say? He isn't here,

dear boy. He should be preparing for the Carantoc Gladiator Games near the main building. His number was picked, but you won't get anywhere near there. Besides, I would watch your back. I am sure someone knows you are snooping around here. Didn't you see Ceiro-Eira and Valmai almost sniff you out?" Caledfryn says, acting worried, afraid of being punished again.

"Head up the spiral staircase. There should be another hallway where they keep the gladiators waiting. There is a dormer window you can crawl through and sneak into the colosseum from the roof. Make sure you do not fall off into the moat; there are demons that lurk near there. Their favorite dish is Diablo Arches who are thrown off the castle as a simple game of fun and trickery.

If they have a taste of your human flesh, I am sure they will go crazy, so watch out," Caledfryn says, backing away into the shadow behind him to lie down, following dungeon rules.

Caledfryn's body disappears in the shadow, for he doesn't want to escape. He doesn't have a lionface head, so he knows he will never be accepted in any populated region of the Death of Ages.

"Go now, boy. Save us all from this hell. It's about time for us to have some action around here. I am sure I will hear the stories of your great victories throughout the ages. We have already heard of your victory killing of Miniver and Cynhafar. You know, that sent shockwaves throughout the House of Cynfor, for we never knew the day would come when a boy descendant from the House of Hartwell would lead the people in Selwyn's Chancer to freedom." Caledfryn says his last words before remaining quiet in the shadows.

Tim, not sure what to say, puts his fist over his chest, showing respect, then rushes out toward the spiral staircase that will lead in the direction of Hynwyn Reese. Tim is hoping he can meet him before he has to fight.

Tim walks through a few doors using the power of the Galon and freezes a few Cynfor guards on the way who were sitting at a room-sized table playing cards and drinking a special liqueur called Cya. Tim continues to run through the halls, trying not to be noticed. At the same time, his mind keeps thinking about his mother, Mary, and of Ceri being the watcher of the Last Fairy Maze Forest. He even thinks about his legendary trainer, Brutus of Troy, as he makes it up the spiral staircase inside the circular turret.

A path with two hallways splits toward the second level of the main building where there are two Cynfor Gatekeeper guards watching an arched door. Tim can hear chants coming from outside, which must mean guests from all over the outer regions of the Death of Ages and above are filling the colosseum.

Tim looks at one guard who has a large iron skeleton key on the side of his metal locking belt, which is attached to the lower part of his iron chestplate. The Cynfor coat of arms is engraved on the chestplate. Both guards are carrying razor-sharp weapons, so Tim decides to not make a huge scene and freezes time with the magical power of the 1st Galon. He walks over to the Gatekeeper with the iron skeleton key and lifts it off his belt while he is frozen in time.

Without wasting a second, the young wizard opens the huge arched door and walks right into the large holding room that has orange light glaring inside, which quickly turns to blue as the day cycle changes once more. Tim notices a gap at the edge of the colosseum that's in clear view through the window. He looks up toward a large, muscular scorpion male figure standing near a large window; he has one human hand and one scorpion claw. Since his time is limited, Tim begins to speak with urgency, knowing the Carantoc Gladiator Games will begin at any moment.

"Hynwyn Reese, my name is Tim from the House of Hartwell, son of Mary. I have come a long way traveling with Brutus of Troy and speaking with Goddess Diana, even meeting the House of Scorpus who were kind enough to help us get here."

"Us, you say? Where is the other?" Hynwyn says with a deep voice.

"Brutus of Troy is the only reason I even knew the Death of Ages existed," says Tim. "But getting back to the point, my friend, Ceri, the last bloodline of the House of Gwynwell, has swallowed the Gwenwyna poison with me to get down here, but she is now the watcher of the Last Fairy Maze

Forest. I need your help, I need to save her now."

"If what you say is true, then there is nothing that can save your friend. If Brutus helped you get here, there is only one thing I can tell you: Leave this place immediately. If you are the boy descendant of the Galon, the best thing for you is to escape. For I am surprised you were able to get into the castle so easily. I guess this proves you are who you say you are." Hynwyn takes a few moments to run his human hand over a long, razor-sharp blade he uses to fight in the games. The blade has kept him alive this long, even though he wishes he had lost sometimes.

"Okay, since you are the true bearer of the Galon," Hynwyn continues, "there is one way for you to save your friend, but it might take your destiny in the act. You are too important. My advice is to save your own life. I always knew the House of Gwynwell would help out if the prophecy was true. There is only one person who can save you and that is Goddess Venus, for she carries the answer that can break the spell of the watcher of the Last Fairy Maze Forest."

"Venus?" asks Tim. "I just saw her before I came into this castle. Are you telling me she didn't tell me how to help her then?" Tim scratches his head, not sure why Venus wouldn't help him.

"No, no, no," Hynwyn says, almost whispering his words. "She wanted you to find the only female of the House of Cynfor, the only princess, to be exact. Her name is Nia. She was born human but has the blood of the Cynfor dragon in her veins. You must find a way to get her to fall in love with you, for only her heart in true love can lift the spell over the power that holds the watcher of the Fairy Maze Forest. It was a curse given to her a long time ago from her father that you murdered, Miniver and Cynhafar, who dreaded anyone who would make her fall in love with their human daughter. Princess Nia is the only one from the House of Cynfor who can free your friend. After the games, you will have to summon Venus to give you the *"Love of Venus."* Princess Nia's curse forbids her to fall in love. Only that power from Venus can make her do so."

Hynwyn turns around to get a better look at the boy who can change it all. He notices that Tim is carrying the Shield of

Aeneas, and at this he smiles because he is astonished such a magical symbol of power and truth actually exists.

"It looks like you have been very busy," says Hynwyn. "I see you have recovered the shield that can even change human history as you know it, but you must leave immediately. It's almost time for me to head out to kill another beast with my axe. Jump out the dormer window and find your way to see Princess Nia. Venus will show up sooner or later, I am sure of that."

Grabbing a huge axe with his scorpion claw, Hynwyn picks up his helmet that has the House of Scorpus coat of arms on it, which he still wears proudly.

Noises start to come toward the door. Gatekeeper guards outside notice that the previous guards are still frozen. Tim quickly snaps his fingers to unfreeze them, which sends them toppling over each other outside the room. Tim nods toward Hynwyn Reese for his help, for he didn't expect the meeting with him would lead to the answers he was looking for.

Tim mounts the Shield of Aeneas on his back and leaps out the dormer window with all his might, doing a front flip then a back flip, which leaves him standing on top of the main building looking over at the colosseum. He wonders where Princess Nia's private balcony could be.

At this very moment he is tired of it all. Tim misses his mother, Mary, more than ever. He knows her doom will come sooner or later, for somehow he believes she will be captive in the hands of the House of Cynfor

any moment now.

## Love from Venus

White and light-grey cumulus mediocris and stratocumulus castellanus cumulogenitus clouds are hovering above Tim. Dawn is beginning to break across the horizon when Tim looks up and notices

**RA14h41m24.24s D37°57'25.64'**

These are the exact same star coordinates that are once again illuminating the blue sky from the same constellation

100

in Boötes. Tim remembers the last time he saw these coordinates was when he was at the funeral pyre for Lancer's death in Troia Nova.

"Oh, God, hear me now. I am here to fulfill my destiny. I trust my heart and spirit more than ever. I trust Mother Mary to lead me into a world of the unknown. Now I fear my friend and mother may be lost forever. If you grant me the power of courage to stay afloat in times of conflict, I will do nothing but return the favor to my family and my country of Wales," Tim says, rushing over to a cement block that's mounted on top of the roof. He hides from the view of the Cynfor dragons in the Keep Station that are looking over to his location, but they are also distracted as they hear the cheers and the trumpets blaring from the colosseum.

The orchestra's brass fills the skies as the first part of the *Carantoc Gladiator Games* is about to begin. Tim, not waiting for another chance to be seen, unexpectedly looks at a small puddle of water resting on the roof and notices he cannot see his reflection. The magical power of the Shield of Aeneas has given him the power of invisibility.

Tim looks at the skies, for he notices the star from the Boötes constellation is blinking at him, granting him another god-like power.

With his new power, Tim begins his way down the side of the roof to the main building, which leads to an overpass into the colosseum. Tim stands guard as he watches

scratched-away House of Diablo Arches coat of arms on his chestplate.

Juvelian's weapon of choice is none other than a large spiky chain that has a metal triangular tip on the end that he can swing around with ease, connected to the other end of a chain has a large angled blade on the end of it. Juvelian's muscular back has spikes coming out of it, which were surgically implanted by the House of Cynfor just for the games.

Grunoktyn continues to speak with his arms stretched out, pointing toward both opponents.

Tim continues to watch, for he is eager to see what everyone has been talking about. Hynwyn uses magic as well when he fights; he is a true warrior of battle.

107

Grunoktyn returns to the royal box where he sits next to Fyanicrum and Guelia, along with Derilyn and Geulia.

Before the fight begins, Bledri and Tomes stand up to make a special announcement, for they have a special guest who will be sitting next to them to watch the games.

"To all of the House of Cynfor and other special invited guests. We have the mother of the last boy descendant of the House of Hartwell in our very presence. Bring her out now!" Bledri orders his personal guards to bring out Tim's mother, Mary.

Tim, on the other side, puts his hands on the edge of the balcony, wanting to scream at the top of his lungs in agony that his very mother is finally paying the price for what she has done. He now can see that she should never have given him the 1st Galon Key, that she is now paying her life for. Tim becomes filled with rage as he ignites the *Firewyn spell* on both of his arms to try and kill the rulers of Cynfor while still remaining invisible. Tim has the perfect aim without his mother being caught in the way as she is brought out and chained to the wall to watch the games on Bledri and Tomes' balcony. A voice speaks to Tim and female hands grip his wrist, stopping him from attacking.

"This is not the right time to save your mother," Goddess Venus says, standing right next to him, invisible to everyone except Tim. He is a tad confused, wondering why he can't avenge his mother,.

"They are too powerful together, my dear boy. Your mother is under the spell of Selwyn's Chancer now," Venus says as she takes a small diamond-shaped box from her sheer dress. Venus whispers a few words into the box, making it illuminate around the edges with a pink light. Venus places the box in Tim's hand, instructing him on what he needs to do at this moment.

"Follow the words of Hynwyn Reese, for he already told you the route you need to take."   Tim looks up at her, his eyes shedding a few tears for his mother.

"This is the **"Love of Venus."** Give this to Princess Nia," says Venus. "Once you do she will fall in love with you. This is the only way to save her, for Ceri will be crucial in escaping the Death of Ages, but it will take longer than you think to achieve this goal. Trust me as you did Diana, Henry, and Lancer Gwynwell, especially your trainer, Brutus of Troy.

"Goddess Diana has already informed me that your emotions are starting to take over. Don't make the same mistake of moving before you are supposed to. Many heroes have died in the path by doing so, including Julius Caesar. Take his life as an example. If Caesar were never assassinated, Rome wouldn't have had its first emperor, Augustus. Everything happens the way it is supposed to. Life has its challenges, and even the smallest steps in the wrong direction can change everything," Venus says before she disappears.

Movement behind the drapes

pushes the drapes forward. Tim moves to the side, noticing Princess Nia walking into her observation balcony. She has beautiful blond hair, with blue eyes that resemble a tropical sea. Tim is amazed by her every movement.

Princess Nia sits down, right next to him without her knowing. She waves for her guards to leave and stand guard outside in the hallway.

On the opposite side of her location, Bledri notices she has entered so he throws a white cloth down into the arena to start the match; he never starts until she is in attendance.

Juvelian dashes toward Hynwyn Reese. Tim looks down at the action. It seems like they are moving in slow motion, getting closer and closer. Juvelian swings his spiked chain toward Hynwyn, who does a backward flip as the tip of Juvelian's blade barely misses his back as he lands a few feet away. The blade swinging through the air gets stuck in a large stone used for defensive purposes during the games.

Hynwyn, taking notice of the moment, leaps high into the air and throws his axe toward Juvelian. The axe has a magical seeking ability that will find its opponent no matter where that opponent stands. The sharp axe slices through Juvelian's thigh, leaving his body slumped over in agonizing pain.

The crowd cheers, for Hynwyn has wounded his opponent with ease. The trumpets blare with each step Hynwyn makes toward Juvelian's body. He looks down at Juvelian who is huffing and puffing while he screams out for mercy with his bloody hand in the air. Hynwyn faces Bledri and Tomes, awaiting their approval for a quick kill. Bledri points his hand downward. Hynwyn takes his sword, thrusting it into the body of Juvelian, leaving his body lifeless.

The crowd goes crazy once more, cheering on the champion who never loses. Bledri whispers something in Tomes' ear about Stratford being on his way into the colosseum without their prior notification. Bledri waves toward the crowd for the next match to start. The Cynfor guards raise the metal gate to escort Hynwyn back into the dungeon. Bledri and Tomes don't want Hynwyn around when Stratford shows up.

At the same time, two other guards grab the body of Juvelian, dragging him back through the metal gate before it completely shuts.

Back inside Princess Nia's observation balcony, Tim places the **_"Love of Venus"_** diamond-shaped box on the bench where Princess Nia is sitting as she watches the eight-on-eight battle. Princess Nia turns and notices the box sitting on the bench. She quickly turns around to see who placed it there but sees no one in sight. She picks up the box and looks at its shape from eye level.

Princess Nia slides open the top of the box, but it only opens halfway. She lightly shakes the box and hears a whisper in her ear. In a flash, a pink light covers the entire royal box without anyone in the colosseum knowing. A body double has been placed in her spot when she and Tim magically appear in an oasis in the desert of the Death of Ages.

Princess Nia awakens a few minutes later, not exactly sure what happened. She looks toward Tim, standing right above her.

Princess Nia rubs her eyes, which sparkle, for the **"Love of Venus"** has made her fall in love with Tim as soon as she laid eyes on him. She runs over to Tim, who is wearing royal clothing from the early 1900s, and wraps her arms around him

"Oh, my love, I have found you. Tell me you love me so I can assure my heart to sing back to you," Princess Nia says. Her emotions have completely taken over her mind and heart by hearing Venus' voice coming from the diamond-shaped box.

Nia is wearing a white linen dress and is holding Tim as tight as she can. Tim, unsure how to react, utters the words she must hear.

"You have found me, I am yours, my love," Tim replies, as they walk over to the pond and sit to speak some more. Food appears next to them. A white unicorn appears too, walking into the oasis. Somehow it has managed to travel down into the Death of Ages. The unicorn gallops over to the pond for a drink of water as Princess Nia begins to speak.

"Oh, look, my love. A beautiful horse from the gods. What a true sign of passion coming toward our presence."

Tim starts thinking about his mother and Ceri, feeling quite awkward about this entire situation. But staying true to his word and believing in Goddess Venus, he gives in to love Princess Nia.

Without them knowing, the twin Wyvern gargoyles, Alfred and Verlock, appear on the opposite side of the pond behind a bush, looking at the new romance unfold before their very eyes.

"Goddess Venus has become involved now. How can this be? I wonder what Stratford will think about the gods interfering with his parallel world and devious plans," Verlock says to his brother.

"It looks like the gods favor the young wizard after all, but we will see," Alfred says, watching the unicorn drink more of the pond water from the oasis. The Wyverns both look toward Princess Nia and Tim speaking to each other on the other side of the pond, wondering what her fathers, Bledri and Tomes, will think about their new love affair.

"We better get out of here. Stratford will get the best of us if we don't report back to him soon," Alfred says, snapping his fingers twice, making them disappear into thin air.

Back at the Carantoc Colosseum, Stratford makes his way into the main royal box where Bledri and Tomes are sitting. Stratford is dressed in full royal-portrait clothing, resembling something King George VI would have worn during his time of reign.

"I see you have captured Mother Mary," Stratford says, walking over to her but not liking the way they have her chained up like an animal. "You imbeciles. Is this how you treat her?" Stratford, for some reason, acts with compassion, possibly because he is a new father with children who could inherit the same power Tim Hartwell has achieved through Selwyn's Chancer. With a wave of his hand, Stratford magically turns the stone bench Mother Mary is sitting on into a plush couch, also turning Mary's clothes from 21st century into a 13th-century red, plush, luxurious long dress. Bledri and Tomes are looking, wondering why Stratford is being so generous to Mother Mary who is supposed to be captive by their liking.

"My lord, we have done as you asked,

but for some reason we have not found Tim Hartwell anywhere within the Death of Ages," Bledri says to Stratford, trying to explain some of their failure of the day.

"That boy is around here somewhere. You must find him immediately! I don't care what it takes," Stratford says as Mary looks at him, still not saying a word. "You should have never given Tim the 1st magical Galon, Mary. You will have to pay sooner or later, but not now. I want you to see him die right in front of you."

Cheers rise from the crowd as another beast is killed in the battle area. Stratford is wearing his large pink and yellow Emosiwn Melyn coronet around his head. Bledri looks at Stratford with his eyes glaring.

"Master, why not have Tim fight

against Hynwyn Reese? When we capture him, it would be the ultimate battle in your honor," Tomes says with his slurred voice. Stratford, amazed, whips his neck around.

"Now that is one of the best ideas I have heard in a long time. You better watch yourself, Bledri. Tomes may be smarter than you think," Stratford says, loosening up, adding some humor before heading back to the Alynn dragon in the upper levels of Selwyn's Chancer where Amelia is taking care of their new twins. Just before Stratford leaves, he turns around and reminds the rulers of the House of Cynfor to not put Amelia in the dungeon but in the secret watchtower.

Bledri and Tomes nod their heads as Stratford disappears into thin air. Mary looks on with disgust, for she can't wait to find a way to escape the castle herself.

　　While Bledri and Tomes are distracted, Mary picks up a nail that Stratford left her on purpose, for some reason. She thinks another plan is going to be taking place very soon. She quickly slips the nail under the sleeve of her dress without anyone noticing. Bledri waves his arms in a motion for the Gatekeeper guards to take her away to the secret watchtower of the castle.

Mary's Escape

Patches of cumulus mediocris and stratocumulus castellanus cumulogenitus clouds are gliding above Princess Nia and Tim, who are still sitting next to the pond as the white unicorn finishes drinking the water from the pond. Goddess Venus, resting on a cloud high above, is looking down at their every move, making sure Tim Hartwell is doing what he needs to do to fulfill his destiny, which is leaving the Death of Ages in one piece.

124

Venus is happy with her results. She moves her right hand in a waving pattern, which sends the duo back into the *Carantoc Gladiator Games* without anyone at the colosseum noticing. Mother Mary has already been taken back to the secret watchtower. The interior of the room is filled with silk and velvet. She is under lock in key, yet Mary will still plan her escape.

At the colosseum, Princess Nia stands up with Tim, both of them visible to the crowd, except no one has noticed yet. She grabs hold of Tim's hand while she screams at the top of her lungs for her father's attention.

**"Father!!!!!"**

The entire crowd, including the fighters on the battleground, stop moving as if something has gone wrong. Bledri and Tomes look toward their daughter's booth, noticing the person they have been looking for all along is holding hands with their very own Princess. Bledri is furious. He goes into survival instinct, roaring loudly for all his guards to run over toward his daughter's balcony, thinking she is about to be harmed in some way.

In a matter of seconds, every Gatekeeper available makes his way toward Princess Nia's private booth. Fyanicrum and Jupira are one of the first ones there, holding large swords directly toward the intruder. Derilyn and Geulia have been waiting a lifetime to marry Princess Nia, even though she is a human girl, even though she has been promised to Fyanicrum and Jupira before Miniver and Cynhafar died.

"What is this? Grab hold of the carrier of the Galon, now!" Fyanicrum says, displeased to see Princess Nia holding Tim's hand as if they were a matched pair.

"What is this madness? Are you siding with a Hartwell now?" Fyanicrum says, ordering Princess Nia to provide some answers as he points his finger toward her out of rage and madness. Everyone in the entire colosseum looks on, shocked, as Fyanicrum is totally out of line.

Bledri and Tomes finally make their way through the crowd. Everyone in the colosseum, including the gladiators still alive on the battleground, are looking over at Princess Nia's balcony.

Bledri has heard enough of Fyanicrum

speaking recklessly toward their daughter. Bledri and Tomes grab Fyanicrum and Jupira by the necks and toss them over the edge of the balcony, making them smash onto the battleground of the colosseum. Due to their size, they are only left with scratches and bruises as they stumble back to their razor sharp feet.

"Everyone, leave the colosseum immediately, the Carantoc games are over. Fyanicrum, you and Jupira will head toward the *Snowyn* Mountains for more ice. Derilyn and Geulia, you will depart for the *Emosiwn* Mountains, and make sure those prisoners mine double the minerals, or else!" Bledri and Tomes say, stomping their foot on the concrete floor.

The entire crowd leaves the Carantoc

Gladiator Colosseum as fast as they can; no one wants to disappoint their rulers. Bledri looks over his shoulder for Ceiro-Eira and Valmai, ordering them to fetch Hynwyn Reese and bring him back down to the colosseum. Bledri looks at Tim with a Shield on his back, but not knowing that it's the same shield from Aeneas of Troy.

Tomes, with his deep voice, orders a few Gatekeepers to bring some Cya to drink at the royal box. Bledri and Tomes are eager to speak with Tim instead of killing him right away, only they truly fear what is about to come next.

As everyone returns to the royal box, Tim begins to ask a few questions before the royal Cynfor leaders can.

"Where is my mother?"

Bledri and Tomes remain silent, looking at Princess Nia holding Tim's hand and not letting it go. Their minds are racing, wondering why she is so affectionate toward the young wizard.

"We are bound to keep Mary at our castle. There is nothing you can do to help her now. Why do you ask these questions? You should know the answer to your riddles, dear boy," Bledri says, answering with a calm voice.

Princess Nia has fallen deeply in love with Tim, despite their young age. Nia has chosen a mate for a marriage that all thought would never happen.

"Father, I have chosen Tim Hartwell to be my husband, for I will love him with all my heart and bear his children at the right age in Cynfornia. He will be my King, for when you and Tomes pass, I will lead our kingdom to the far edges of the Death of Ages," she says.

"Arrrgh!" Bledri says as his tail whips down a bench behind him. They know they have no other choice, for it has been written in stone in the **Royal Cynforian Chapel** by their father, Miniver and Cynhafar. Once Princess Nia chooses a mate there is no reversing it. Bledri and Tomes have to accept their daughter's wishes, provided to her since birth.

"My precious daughter, how can you do this to us? Stratford runs Selwyn's Chancer. He will declare war upon us if we allow such blasphemy," Bledri says, pleading with her while he cracks his knuckles in anguish.

"You have heard my words loud and clear. You will marry us at once and send us to the *Bluebells Forest* in Cynfornia. If you decline, I will release the *Soulsynwn dragon* and the vines from the Last Fairy Maze Forest to destroy this castle," Princess Nia says, making threats toward her father, for the **"Love of Venus"** has her heart and mind locked on her decision.

Bledri and Tomes, nervous, sweating from their heads, pick up a large cup filled with Cya juice to help them ease their fears of the wrath of Stratford. They both know the combined power of the fairy watcher and the Soulsynwn dragon can be even worse for them.

Bledri and Tomes look over at Tim, not saying a word just yet but knowing they have to agree with her terms. The Senate Hall will surely convince them otherwise if they do not. Because of the love for their daughter, they must agree with her terms.

The Gatekeepers have finally brought Hynwyn Reese out to the center of the battleground. He looks around, wondering why the entire colosseum is completely empty. Bledri makes a few decisions to ease his anger.

"Guards, send Hynwyn Reese to the Last Fairy Maze Forest. Make him suffer for the pain I must endure by accepting my daughter's proposal. Someone must be punished and I choose him," Bledri says.

Tim looks down at Hynwyn in the center of the colosseum, sad that he can do nothing to save him. The Gatekeepers shove Hynwyn in the middle of his back as hard as they can. They push him toward the back of the castle, which leads to the Last Fairy Maze Forest. Bledri, smiling while Hynwyn is being pushed along, turns his neck around, looking at Tomes. They both look down at their daughter and Tim Hartwell and continue to speak.

"I accept your proposal on the premise of Tim fighting with us against Stratford and the House of Diablo Arches when the time comes. We hope he knows war will come sooner or later," Bledri says. He drinks more of the Cynforian Cya juice with its blue color that is extracted. The Bluebells Forest resembles Dockey Wood, Ashridge in England.

"I will fight with you," Tim says.

134

The Galon is beginning to take over his emotions a little more each day. They all toast to the new fiancé of their princess. Then, one of the Gatekeepers comes running back with his arm bleeding badly. Bledri and Tomes stand up, wondering exactly what happened.

"Explain yourselves, you fools," Bledri says.

"Your highness, Mother Mary has escaped from the tower. She has killed some of the Gatekeepers who were transporting Hynwyn to the forest. Some horses grew from the ground, splitting in two. Mother Mary and Hynwyn rode off into the Last Fairy Maze Forest. We tried to close the Gates of Death in time, but they both escaped," the Gatekeeper explains.

"You must be joking. How did this happen? How did she escape?" Tomes says.

"Let them be. We have bigger issues at hand," Bledri says.

Tim is smiling, happy that his mother at least escaped with someone who can protect her while in the Last Fairy Maze Forest.

"Order the ceremony at once!" Bledri says, still enraged that Tim has killed their father, Miniver and Cynhafar, but what can they do now but accept the changes of the events at hand.

The only thing Tim isn't aware of is that the blood of Amelia's bite still runs through Ceri's veins. Once she gets wind of his marriage to Princess Nia, Ceri will be furious, even though Princess Nia controls the land she has been cursed to live in forever.

Mother Mary and Hynwyn Reese, who are already lost inside the Last Fairy Maze Forest, begin looking for a way out. Luckily, Hynwyn knows of a secret path back into the castle, if they can find it.

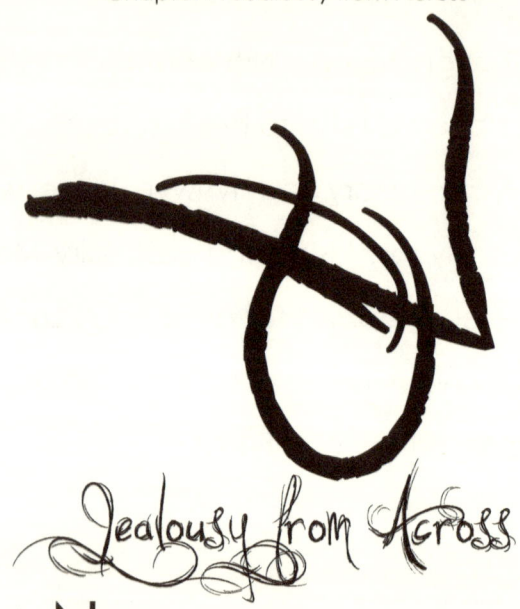

Jealousy from Across

Night has fallen across Snowdon, in North Wales. The Alynn dragon, which holds the Amelia fortress inside the belly of the dragon, is flying high above cumulonimbus clouds where lightning strikes, beating the sky. Rain pours on the shoulders of Stratford, who is watching the rain drop into the Llyn Cwellyn reservoir in front of him. The rain is cold as it bounces off his Emosiwn Melyn coronet around his head. Lylock and his son, Baron Milwr, are standing next to Stratford. Amelia remains resting in her chambers inside the Alynn dragon, which is making a circular pattern above more cumulonimbus clouds that approach their location.

The entire House of Diablo Arches stands behind the three of them, dressed in full battle armor with the House of Diablo Arches coat of arms on their chestplates, helmets, and weaponry.

"It's time, Lylock. Are you ready to take charge and bring me the heads of Bledri and Tomes? You and your armies will storm the walls of the House of Cynfor. Leave nothing but dust for you to rebuild your realm. You will regain control of the Caves of Siôr diamond trade," Stratford says, standing in human form but with his head in beast form.

"I am ready, my lord. We will crush them with all our might. We will not fail you. I have been waiting to retake our place in the Death of Ages, controlling the dungeon of dead spirits once more."

Baron Milwr speaks to his soldiers, who are wearing Emosiwn Melyn diamonds to protect themselves from his deadly voice.

"My soldiers, we are ready to attack. We will enter the east Gates of Death that lead into the colosseum. They will never expect us." Baron is unaware that the House of Cynfor is ready for war.

Stratford, among the crowds near Llyn Cwellyn, has already foreseen victory. In his mind, he thinks about helping Mary escape. He doesn't want her killed just yet. Not until the Book of Hartwell has been opened. Stratford is aware of Mary's escape with Hynwyn Reese. He is very disappointed in Alfred and Verlock for not giving him all the information about Goddess Venus interfering with his plans. "Those bloody Wyverns," he says, looking at the rain hitting the water below his feet.

At twilight, Stratford uses his power to send the House of Diablo Arches through a portal that will lead them directly into the Death of Ages instead of traveling through the House of Scorpus hoist. Lylock and Baron Milwr swing their arms for their army to move out. Some of the Diablo Arches ride their Diablo black horses into the light of the portal. Stratford whistles for the Alynn dragon to swoop back down from the sky as the army moves through the magic portal.

The Alynn dragon lands back on the ground, opening its enormous mouth. The dragon's bottom jaw lays flat on the ground. Stratford walks into the mouth of the dragon, which then heads back into the cumulonimbus clouds above, disappearing in the mist of the dark night.

Darron and Darryn, who are eating in the *Hall of Judgement*, hear word from their Scorpus soldiers that war has been declared on the House of Cynfor. Darron, along with Darryn, laugh as hard when they hear the news. As long as it's not them, they couldn't care less. They have always been nonchalant and callous toward other House affairs.

Back down in the Death of Ages, inside the Cynforian chapel, Senate members are sitting behind *Preacher Ifor* and his lionface *Vaughn*, who is waiting at the mantle for the ceremony of marriage to begin. Cynforian ball music is flowing through the chapel. A long aisle with luxurious carpet and drapes also flows through the chapel walls. Everyone with importance to the royal House of Cynfor is watching the ceremony, waiting for Princess Nia to walk down the aisle.

The Cynforian marriage bell-clock rings loudly inside the chapel. Preacher Ifor holds the bridal scroll with both hands as the bell-clock winds down. The bells leave a middle-pitch ringing sound, serving as a marker for the bride to walk into the chapel.

Everyone inside the chapel turns around to look at Princess Nia, who is wearing a beautiful wedding gown that is designed from a high-end taffeta organza. The appliques that bloom down the hem have been stitched with perfection.

The ringing of the bridal music dies down as Princess Nia walks down the royal aisle at a steady pace, with young captured fairies from the Maze Forest holding the hem of her dress.

Tim, in a formal suit resembling George VI from 1945, glances back at Princess Nia; she is more beautiful than he could have ever imagined. He's very nervous, for he knows Ceri was showing her love for him. Now, he almost hates that he was not able to comfort her after she saved his life. Now she is cursed, he thinks to himself, to be the watcher of the Last Fairy Maze Forest. Bledri and Tomes meet their daughter, proudly holding her hand the rest of the way down the royal aisle.

Princess Nia finally makes her way down to Tim. The young wizard holds her hand while they face Preacher Ifor and Vaughn to begin the vows.

Two unexpected guests appear on the side of the chapel but completely invisible to the crowd.

"He must be completely hatstand. Tim must be out of his mind," says Alfred. "I guess the Goddess Venus knows what she is doing, allowing something like this to happen. Who would have known the Princess of Cynfor's engagement would bring an alliance with the House of Hartwell. I don't know what Stratford will do."

"I guess he is not worried," Verlock replies. He looks toward Alfred, who happens to be eating some of the sugar bread displayed on the side of the chapel. Alfred, usually the focused one, loves Cynforian sugar bread cookies more than anything in Selwyn's Chancer.

"How can you find the time to eat? The House of Diablo Arches are on their way toward the castle from the outer regions. They've already taken full control of the Caves of Siôr," Verlock says, smacking the food out of Alfred's mouth, trying to get him to pay attention to the matter at hand.

"I don't know what to say this time. Matter of fact, we should head to the forest and see what Mother Mary and Hynwyn Reese are up to. Hopefully they aren't dead by now," Alfred says. He snaps his fingers, magically sending them into the Last Fairy Maze Forest to see if they are still alive.

Princess Nia and Tim are holding hands as Preacher Ifor finishes his speech before Tim repeats the royal vows.

"I promise to love you, no matter sickness, until death do us part. I do," Tim says. Preacher Ifor looks toward Nia to finish her vows.

"And do you, Nia, promise to love Tim, no matter sickness, until death do you part?" Ifor says, looking toward Princess Nia who has a tear coming from her eye from complete happiness.

"I promise to love you, no matter

sickness, until death do us part. I do," she says.

Preacher Ifor lets Tim know he may put the 20-carat Emosiwn Melyn diamond wedding ring on Nia's finger. Tim slides the ring on her finger and gives her a formal kiss on the mouth.

All of the Cynforian spectators scream with joy. They know the prophecy of her marriage will save their people from Selwyn's Chancer.

Bledri and Tomes, along with the rest of the Senate Hall members, continue to clap their hands with excitement, except for Fyanicrum, Jupira, Derilyn, and Geulia, who are sick to their stomachs with the very notion of Tim becoming second in line to the throne of the House of Cynfor.

Everyone continues clapping while the newly married couple heads for the arched exitway. The royal bell-clock rings only a few times, which marks the end of the wedding ceremony.

A white, beautiful carriage that has yellow and pink Emosiwn Melyn diamonds encrusted on it pulls up to the front of the royal chapel. Princess Nia and her new husband step into the carriage. Tim notices the Shield of Aeneas and the rest of his belonging are inside.

Princess Nia has magic of her own, including the power to lift or move heavy objects with her thoughts. She can also control all things in the Last Fairy Maze Forest, except the mind of the fairy watcher, for that is controlled by Ceri's doomed curse.

Everyone waves to the newly married couple as they travel to the sacred Bluebells Forest in Cynfornia, located at the far end of the Death of Ages. The air is completely different there. No can breathe the air there and stay alive. Only the House of Cynfor's princess and her husband through marriage are allowed to breathe the potent air, which is more poisonous than all of the air in the Death of Ages. This was a fail-safe to protect the future of the Cynfor throne, where a new kingdom will be born.

The royal white carriage makes its way past the northern Gates of Death, entering the unknown region to the Bluebells Forest. Princess Nia and Tim will live there for the next five years and are forbidden to have any sexual contact until their sixteenth birthdays. By ritual, Princess Nia must bear an heir to the throne of the new kingdom, Cynfornia.

Night falls in the Death of Ages. The sky, which has cirrus and cirrostratus clouds, turns a dark blue. Bledri and Tomes are sitting on their thrones, creating a strategic defensive plan for the arrival of the House of Diablo Arches. They are sitting at a round table, which allows all of the Senate Hall, including the royal heirs, to speak together. Bledri and Tomes order metal spikes to be placed all around the castle, as well as a layer of oil that they will ignite once the intruders are outside the walls.

An hour passes by, then the war horn in the Keep Station sends out an alert, noting the intruders are visible from a distance. The frontline Diablo Arches have lit torches coming from their scepters and are marching toward the castle of Cynfor.

One of the mid-level Gatekeepers who escaped the attack on the *Caves of Siôr* has made his way into the main building with a few others, breathing hard, for they were almost killed in the worst possible way.

"Your highness, the House of Diablo Arches have taken over the caves. We have failed you, my lord," the Gatekeeper explains.

"Others managed to escape and are heading toward the *Snowyn* Mountains for refuge," the Gatekeeper continues.

Fyanicrum receives a scroll from his lieutenant from the Keep Station, stating the House of Diablo Arches are approximately eight hundred meters away from their exact location in the castle *(miles: 0.5, meters: 804.672)*.

"Destiny has made our daughter, Princess Nia, save our race. I fear not Stratford anymore. He planned for our removal from the Death of Ages some time ago, we have heard. My brothers, we will fight until the end. We will fight until there are no more. We will win in our hearts no matter what. Do not fear the power of Stratford's Selwyn's Chancer world. We will live on, we will prevail!" Bledri says.

Everyone gets up from their seat, heading for the curtain walls where all of their weapons are mounted. Tons of Cynforian guards load their bows with arrows the size of trees that can take down a large number of enemies at once.

Bledri and Tomes order their entire army to stand guard, waiting for death to approach their castle. Their mission is to protect their throne from annihilation.

Tomes looks out into the night. The moon has parked itself high above altocumulus lenticularis clouds forming in the distance in the shadows above them.

Legions of Diablo black horses are pounding against the rugged ground toward the River Styx. The frontline of Diablo Arches begin their way down to the river.

Lylock and Baron Milwr stand on top of the small hill with their own royal guards. Some of them are holding staffs that carry the flag with the House of Diablo Arches coat of arms glaring in the night, lighting the skies around them.

"Attack!" Lylock screams. They watch the frontlines get closer to the River Styx. Bledri and Tomes, knowing they are completely safe while inside the castle, watch the Diablo Arches mount their camp around the eastern side of the castle.

Bledri orders Derilyn to fetch him the scroll of Charun, allowing them to control the movements and magic of Charun. A special power granted them three wishes from the *psychopompoi* of the underworld.

Derilyn fetches the scroll from the sacred locker in the Keep Station, rushing back over to the ruler for the next plan of attack.

The frontline of the Diablo Arches have parked themselves on the border of the River Styx. Bledri spreads open the scroll, reading the first wish he has been granted from Charun. The scroll was a gift from Charun for giving so many souls that have paid him well during the ages.

Tomes looks at the scroll, along with Bledri, and they read the first wish out loud, which is composed in Welsh dactylic hexameter:

Welsh:

Bydd yr afon yn codi | bydd Tanau llosgi
| Unrhyw eneidiau agosáu | bydd byrddau Troi

~~~~~~~~~~~~~~~~~~~~~~~~~~~~~~~~~~~~~~~~~~~~~~~~

English:

The river will rise | fires will burn
| any approaching souls | Tables will Turn

~~~~~~~~~~~~~~~~~~~~~~~~~~~~~~~~~~~~~~~~~~~~~~~~~~~~~~~~~

Bledri reads the words slowly and carefully. Any mispronounced words will make the wish void. With every word spoken properly, Charun appears from out of the dark night on the Styx, arriving toward the *Port of Charun,* slamming fast into his dock station. The frontline of the Diablo Arches stand there unafraid but with no clue of the aftermath that is awaiting them.

Charun places his oar down and raises his scepter in the air with his right skeleton arm. His left hand rests on the oval handle connected to a rope with the same ancient bell, which he uses to inform the House of Cynfor to open the Gates of Death. This time, Charun grants Bledri and Tomes' first wish.

He stands on his small black ship wearing his torn sheer black robe that drapes over his body. Charun screams in the air, raising his scepter in a swift upward motion toward the sky. The ancient bells ring three times, making the water level of the River Styx rise high into the air, forming the shape of a large hand. Bledri throws a torch, igniting the hand with fire from the oil he had his Gatekeepers put there earlier.

Lylock and Baron Milwr look in fear for the first time in ages. They have never seen magic so dreadful coming from the River Styx. The titan black hand makes fire and the essence of the River Styx pounce on top of the entire frontline of the House of Diablo Arches, destroying them all.

Cheers from dragon vocal cords fill

the skies as they look on while the hand of fire retreats into River Styx. There is silence around the earth, except for the fire burning on the ground where the frontline of the Diablo Arches used to be.

Lylock is looking on, pissed, and accidently kills one of his royal guards by swinging his fist to the side of him.

The House of Diablo Arches gather on the top of the hill, thinking of another plan of attack. They were never expecting to go up against the power of a psychopompoi from the human underworld, Tartarus.

Bledri, smelling fear in his opponent, yells out orders for his Gatekeepers to start shooting tree-trunk-sized arrows toward the hills. The arrows, because of their size, instantly kill more of the Diablo Arches.

The Gatekeepers pull back another set of titan-sized crossbows, sending the arrows flying through the air. Each one of the arrows takes out twenty Diablo Arches with every pull. Baron yells out to his father, Lylock, that they won't last much longer if they don't find a way inside the castle.

Stratford, sitting in one of the royal rooms in Amelia's chamber above the upper levels of Selwyn's Chancer, is playing chess against himself when he senses his Diablo Arches are failing him once more. He gets up and walks outside the castle to the area where the Alynn dragon heart is beating below the glass floor. He ponders a second, thinking of the perfect plan to get the Diablo Arches inside the castle to the House of Cynfor.

"Ceri," Stratford whispers. If he informs her of the marriage of Tim and Princess Nia, she will become enraged from Amelia's very own love potion and tracking potion she infected her with in Troia Nova.

Stratford, smiling from ear to ear with another devious plan, looks over at Sylkin and toward the purple crystal castle inside the belly of the Alynn dragon. Stratford makes his body begin to disappear slowly but stops himself because he forgot to feed Sylkin. The last thing he needs is Sylkin breaking himself free because of his hunger and killing his wife and new kids. He magically makes a Tyrannosaurus appear for his pet to eat. Sylkin pounces on the dinosaur, shredding it to pieces like he always does.

Stratford, almost forgetting, claps his

hands in front of him, making his snitches, Verlock and Alfred, appear in front of him.

"I should kill you both where you stand. How would you think you could keep any secret from me," Stratford says, smacking them both in the face.

"We were going to tell you, my lord, but...," Verlock mumbles.

Stratford burns Verlock's right arm, making the Wyvern scream in agony. Alfred rushes to the floor to aid his twin brother. Stratford burns Alfred as well, this time on the right leg. Alfred screams as his body rolls over Verlock in pain, leaving them both sorry for ever helping Tim at all.

"I should have killed you both. You are very lucky I need you. The Diablo Arches have failed me once more in the Death of

Ages. I might have to rethink their power in my world," Stratford says, walking over to the Alynn heart, which is beating below the glass floor.

"Both of you will travel to wherever those newlyweds are and inform me of what they're doing. Don't fail me again or I will make that pain last for an eternity," Stratford says. He claps his hands once, making the twin Wyvern gargoyles vanish into thin air, back into the Death of Ages.

Before Stratford goes back into the depths of his parallel world, he looks up at the balcony of Amelia's Chamber where he notices his wife, Amelia, standing. She is holding one of his newborns, Cayne, in her arms. Amelia's body double, the spirit Megan Lynelle, is holding his daughter,

Amelia II. Stratford transports his athletic body through the air, landing on the balcony next to them. Stratford's face lights up like a candle with a father's joy, even with the madness down in the Death of Ages. He takes his son from Amelia's arms, holding him high in the air. Below, Sylkin roars with his animal instinct, happy for them as well.

Megan Lynelle merges her spirit back into Amelia's body and makes Amelia hold her daughter in her arms. Amelia uses her magic to make the ancient piano play a sweet tune for the newborns. Both babies fall back to sleep in their parents' arms.

For the first time, Stratford has more chaos than ever in Selwyn's Chancer, but he is happy in his heart, bearing heirs to the throne of his kingdom as well.

## When A Kingdom Falls

Rain begins to pour from the low-level nimbostratus and stratocumulus clouds high above the Last Fairy Maze Forest. The raindrops hit the leaves, creating natural melodies of water dripping off tree branches throughout the forest. Mother Mary and Hynwyn Reese are riding Jupiter's horses down a path through the maze.

Mary looks over to Hynwyn still wearing his armor. He stops in a section of the path as his ears pick up sounds from the right side of the forest. He raises his hand in the air, letting Mary know that someone is following them. Hynwyn unsheathes a sword he was able to steal from a Gatekeeper back at the castle. Hynwyn, unafraid of death, yells into the forest, wanting this mysterious figure to reveal its identity.

"Show yourself. I can hear your footsteps. No need to pretend, we know you are following us," he says. A twig on the ground snaps in the darkness. Mother Mary and Hynwyn look fast, for they see the fairy watcher. Ceri has been following them. As the watcher, she was able to hear them riding when they first arrived.

The fairy watcher begins to speak to them. Mary looks at Ceri's face poking through a key-shaped coat of arms mounted on one of the trees.

"What are you doing in my precious realm? I am very surprised to hear the sounds of the mother of the son who carries the Galon," she says. Ceri sniffs the air. She can identify both of them even though she is blind.

"Ceri Gwynwell, or should I say Zoe Beckham from Greenhill. I see you have been cursed to be the watcher of this dreadful forest," Mother Mary says. Sad for Ceri, a few tears fall down Mary's face, especially since she is the last bloodline to the House of Gwynwell.

They continue to speak, then another

sound brushes against the beautiful trees back to the right of them as the sky turns from dark orange to midnight blue. Stratford has come to change the order of events. He looks up toward the rain as it graces his face. Stratford raises his right hand in the air, which magically makes the rain stop, but only where they all stand.

"I see both of you met the new fairy watcher. Oh, Mary, I see your son is growing up mighty fast in the Death of Ages. I have heard he is also the prince to the House of Cynfor by marrying Princess Nia. You should be proud of him, Ceri," Stratford says, looking over toward Ceri's face. He walks into the clear path's still, thick mist, gracefully dissolving in different parts of the forest.

Ceri begins to shed tears, even though the trio cannot see her eyes. The love blood potion injected by Amelia has infected her train of thought. Enraged, Ceri makes the wind pick up all around the forest. Vines on the trees begin to come alive, moving, stretching throughout the forest. Some of the trees begin to grow even bigger from the roots bursting from the wet ground.

Ceri, hearing of Tim's marriage, thinks they are hidden in the castle of the House of Cynfor. Her mind is struck with revenge at the thought of confronting Princess Nia and Tim. She believes Tim was supposed to give her love forever.

"I will kill them both, I will have my revenge. I will end the life of every member of the House of Cynfor if it's the last thing I do," Ceri says, enraged.

Mother Mary and Hynwyn try their best to explain, looking back, noticing Stratford has disappeared. He left them with the wrath of the fairy watcher, knowing they could be killed instantly by the forest coming alive.

Ceri's face inside the coat of arms disappears, leaving only the coat of arms on the tree trunk. She morphed into the foursome headed to the castle of Cynfor. Her plans, to bring the forest with her and take down the unbreakable curtain wall, are exactly what Stratford wanted. His plan will not be complete, allowing the House of Diablo Arches to invade the castle all at once.

The forest is making so much noise,

170

and each tree is stretching toward the castle. The path where Mother Mary and Hynwyn are standing is closing by the minute. They head toward a tunnel that leads underground. It was an escape route for Princess Nia to leave the castle in case the day ever came for the House of Cynfor to save their race by sending her away.

"Mary, there is a tree with a blue heart that illuminates. We must find it immediately! This tunnel leads underground. It will take us back to the castle. Follow me," Hynwyn says.

They ride their horses to a certain part of the forest. The wind continues to blow strong and the mist blocking their vision makes it hard for them to find the tunnel. The rain pours even harder. Mary's red dress, which Stratford made for her, magically turns back to the 21st-century clothes she was wearing back in Tenby.

As they continue riding, Hynwyn notices blue streams of light coming from a section of the forest. And they both notice a blue heart on a dark brown tree, with a blue rose growing from one of the branches. As they get closer, they can see the blue heart illuminating, blinking on and off slowly as it fades in and out on the bark of the huge tree.

"This is it!" Hynwyn says as he walks over to the tree, which is moving slowly. He takes his hand and presses it gently on the tree with the right amount of pressure. A path of light appears below their feet, outlining a large box the size of an ordinary room in a home.

Behind them, Hynwyn notices tons of trees moving toward them and loud thumping sounds. The same beast that tried to kill Tim while he was in the forest is coming their way. The ground below sinks down to an angled driveway, making a ramp that leads into a circle tunnel below the ground. Little do they know war is waiting for them as soon as they arrive at the castle.

As they ride into the opening of the lowered path, Hynwyn turns around, noticing a large dragon leaping toward them, trying to kill him. The mouth of the dragon is huge, but Hynwyn's long blade slides through the side of its mouth. The dragon beast shoots a small amount of fire out of its mouth. Hynwyn, using his Scorpus claw, shields himself from the dragon's fire. Without the beast's knowledge, three large trees come to the side of the dragon. Tree branches and vines cocoon the entire dragon within seconds. Hynwyn, on his horse, shoots down into the tunnel behind Mother Mary as the ground begins to lift. They can hear sounds of the dragon, which is in agony. The ground completely shuts off any light from above their heads but keeps them safe from the forest destroying everything above ground.

The moisture is thick down in the tunnel, which is pitch black. Hynwyn is searching for something to make a torch with.

*"Fymru Nacht spell,"* Mary whispers. Her mother, Lily, taught her how to make fire using an ancient spell from the House of

Hartwell. Only females from the House can summon such power if they ever use the 1st Galon, a secret her son, Tim, never knew.

Hynwyn looks at Mary with one of her arms covered in light-pink flame. "Mother of God, how do you know such magic?" Hynwyn asks.

"In time you will know more about the Galon, but for now we need to get out of this place. Which way do we go?" Mary asks.

The path they ride on is made from hard dirt reinforced with iron to hold its shape over the ages.

"Somehow, I truly believe Selwyn's Chancer is becoming more alive even without Stratford's knowing," Mary says, heading through the underground damp passage.

They can still hear the earth moving above. Mary thinks about how Ceri had completely lost it when they saw her earlier. A distant light peeks from the tunnel ahead. Jupiter's horse that Mary is riding snorts, sensing danger in the tunnel. The horse senses someone else in the tunnel.

A goblin named *Phylip Prysorwen* is waiting for them to come farther into the tunnel. His favorite food is horses, and he hasn't had one in a long time.

"Come, my guests, come give me what I want," Prysorwen says. He will not let them pass until they give up their horses.

Prysorwen hates light. His body is the color green. Warts cover his upper torso, and he has small legs. Phylip Prysorwen can only walk with his arms and his hairy fists that help him throughout the tunnel. His body smells like old milk. He doesn't like water or washing one bit. His hair used to be blond but is now almost dark brown-black from the dirt and fungus growing in it.

Prysorwen has elf-shaped ears and sharp teeth. Many of his teeth are missing or broken off from decay. He doesn't wear a shirt, only black cargo pants that stop at his knees. His leather-strap boots are so worn that his dirty toes stick out the front of them.

Prysorwen used to be part of the House of Diablo Arches, but after his body was deformed from sleeping with a witch in the outer region, he was locked in the dungeon. He was then ordered to dig the tunnel and a small room for him to remain there. His only purpose was to maintain the tunnel in case Princess Nia ever needed to escape.

Phylip Prysorwen moves by animal instinct. He continues to demand his new guests give him their horses as he slides over to another part of the tunnel, unexpectedly fixing and repairing it right in front of them.

Hynwyn looks at Mary and raises his eyebrows. They both think Phylip Prysorwen is out of his mind from seclusion in the tunnel. They continue to watch him move throughout the tunnel, fixing different parts of the iron braces and locks. He leaves multiple different tools in various areas of the tunnel, due to his short memory.

Prysorwen keeps a dirty tan cloth in his pocket, using it to squeeze the dirt from underneath his fingernails every time he finishes a segment of the tunnel.

Mary raises her hand, which is still illuminated from the *Fymru Nacht spell*. The light-pink fire annoys Prysorwen, who is holding his hand in front of his eyes, blocking the fire illumination.

"Fire, fire, get away, fire, leave fire be, leave fire, away," Prysorwen says with his high-pitched voice. He notices more water leakage in part of the tunnel beside him. Mother Mary taps Hynwyn on the shoulder, pointing toward the side of Prysorwen's pants. There is a scratched-away House of Diablo Arches coat of arms, which is almost completely faded.

Mother Mary, knowing they don't have much time, tries to speed things along

179

by informing Prysorwen that they need to pass. Prysorwen is stubborn in his own way since the only food in the tunnel is the rats that manage to find their way from the castle into the tunnel passageway.

"No pass, give me those horse, I will let you pass then. Only if horses I keep," Prysorwen says. He demands that they give him something he doesn't even own. Mary, not feeling his offer, makes a proposition of her own.

"Look, you, we need to pass now. Why do you keep blocking us from going on our way?" she says.

Phylip Prysorwen, ignoring them, continues working on the tunnel as if he didn't hear what she said, even though he did. "Only Princess Nia tell me what to do.

Only Princess Nia allowed to travel through tunnel. No one allowed to travel through tunnel, only Princess Nia," Prysorwen says with his sporadic way of speaking.

The instincts of Jupiter's horses come into play. Their eyes begin to charge with electricity as if they are about to kill Prysorwen. He is frightened by the horses' eyes and he goes from hungry to not hungry at all. He begins to change his mind, deciding to let his guests pass.

Mary, liking the horses taking charge, begins to pet the side of each horse, thanking them for helping. Prysorwen jumps back to the side of the tunnel when they go by. He accidently breaks one of the brackets to a long metal beam that holds part of the tunnel together. Water splashes all over him, which makes him paranoid. He believes he will be punished for not fixing the brackets. He jumps to his feet with his clothes soaking wet, attending to any part of the broken bracket that needs fixing. Mary and Hynwyn pass by, leaving Phylip Prysorwen to tend to what he has broken. Mother Mary and Hynwyn Reese continue down the path, laughing at what they just encountered. They had never met such a foolish and crazy goblin-type creature in their lives.

They finally make it to the end of the tunnel, which leads to a circular iron door with twenty-three locks. Mother Mary looks over toward Hynwyn with her eyes wide.

"So how do we plan on getting in? There are so many locks," Mary says.

Hynwyn jumps off his horse and walks over to the doorway. He examines each lock carefully. Using his Scorpus claw, he snaps the first one with ease. Mary looks on with amazement. She doesn't have magic strong enough to break Cynforian metal.

"I don't think I ever would have thought of that first," says Mary, smiling. Hynwyn continues to break each one of the huge locks. Each has the House of Cynfor Senate coat of arms on it, since it was their idea to create the tunnel for Princess Nia's safety.

"On the other side of the wall, there should be a hidden room leading underneath the main bailey near the main building of the castle. We will have to run inside the *Snowyn Chamber* and gather all the supplies we can from one of the utility rooms. There is only one place we can survive in the outer regions of the Death of Ages until we can find a safer route up to the higher regions of Selwyn's Chancer," Hynwyn says. He breaks the last lock on the circular iron doorway. With his human hand he waves for Mary to stand back as he uses his Scorpus claw to pry open the doorway.

Unexpectedly, smoke begins to stream into the tunnel, catching Mary's attention right away. She quickly points down at Hynwyn's feet. The pressure blows the door completely off the large metal hinges.

**BOOOM!**

The door slams past them, almost killing them both as they duck down. Mother Mary and

184

Hynwyn get back on their horses, walking through the destruction. Hynwyn jumps off his horse when inside, noticing the *Snowyn Chamber* is not full of ice. Instead, the entire place is burnt. Everything is destroyed. Black smoke fills the chamber as Mary and Hynwyn look at the aftermath. They wonder what happened, but they can only think of one answer: the Diablo Arches.

All of the dead spirits are screaming to be set free. Their cells are burnt to a crisp, while the prisoners inside are unharmed.

Mary uses her magical **Wyntearia spell**. She blows wind throughout the *Snowyn Chamber*, extinguishing the fire for them to ride through. Hynwyn jumps back on Jupiter's horse, heading outside to safety.

"How did they get in here?" Mary says to Hynwyn, who shrugs his shoulders, thinking the fairy watcher must have knocked down one of the curtain walls for the Diablo Arches to raid the castle grounds.

"Even though the House of Cynfor is smarter and larger, it looks like they have been completely wiped out," Hynwyn says.

Mother Mary turns around, not hearing the horses that have turned themselves into small Emosiwn Melyn diamond chess pieces on the ground. She picks them up, tucking them into the back pocket of her blue jeans.

"Someone purposely destroyed the *Snowyn Chamber*," she says while they continue riding down another huge hallway leading to the outer doors of the dungeon.

Facing the west Gates of Death in the midst of the action, Hynwyn looks over toward Mary with her back on the stone wall, looking outside into the main bailey that is covered in forest.

"It looks like Ceri has made her way in," she says. Bodies of dead Cynfor dragons from all ranks are lying everywhere. Hynwyn knows something is very wrong with this picture.

"How are you able to breathe the air of the Death of Ages? Were you given the Gwenwyna potion like I was by Darron and Darryn?" Hynwyn says. Even speaking their names makes his blood boil from betrayal.

"I am not sure. All I remember is I was painting in my room back in Tenby. The next thing I knew, I felt a hard thump on the back of my head. After that, I remember seeing my feet drag against the floor of this castle, carried by the Gatekeepers to the Carantoc Gladiator Games to meet Bledri and Tomes," she explains. "Only the House of Scorpus has the ability to send living humans from the reality world," she continues.

"I see," Hynwyn replies.

Out of the corner of their eyes, they notice multiple shadows appearing beneath an archway through the stone wall from the lower bailey. They also hear voices.

"Remove all the dead bodies and kill the wounded," Lylock says.

"That is the voice of Lylock," Hynwyn whispers to Mary. "They are inspecting the damage, making sure the area is secure."

Mary and Hynwyn jump back to hide as multiple Diablo Arches on their black horses ride through the main bailey. Some of them are pulling dead bodies into the center to burn in the pyre they made. Baron Milwr walks from behind his father, Lylock, with a pleased grin on his face. He is finally conquering the land that has been ruled by the House of Cynfor for ages.

The forest has knocked down the Gates of Death but hasn't grown anywhere else in the castle. Mary and Hynwyn continue to watch the Diablo Arches with their burning arrows stretched toward Bledri and Tomes, who are shackled by their necks and feet. Bledri and Tomes are badly beaten and cut, while two Cynfor dragons who are walking with the House of Diablo Arches remain unharmed.

"They are Fyanicrum, Jupira, Derilyn, and Geulia, third in line to the throne. They must have betrayed Bledri and Tomes. Everyone knew they both wanted Nia's hand in marriage. I guess this is their revenge," Hynwyn says, whispering to Mary.

Fyanicrum takes his large foot and kicks the face of Bledri, making their entire body fall to the ground on their side.

"Who is your leader now?" Fyanicrum says. His lionface Jupira grins while they cause pain to their prior rulers. They are wearing precious wreaths of pink and yellow Emosiwn Melyn diamond coronets, which keep them safe around Baron Milwr. Lylock walks over to the fallen kings with his hands at his sides. He points toward Fyanicrum to execute their rulers. For sparing their lives, they will  be allowed to live if they show this special measure of good faith.

With their large blades in one hand, Fyanicrum and Jupira walk over to Bledri and Tomes. Fyanicrum looks down at the face of Bledri, who has teeth missing and is coughing up blood. He raises his large blade in the air, which shines off the morning sun. His sword slices though Bledri's and Tomes' heads at once, sending their body rolling over to the wall. Fyanicrum and Jupira walk over, picking up their heads and holding them in the air like trophies.

"You see, my lord, we mean business," Fyanicrum says with huge smile on his face.

Jupira looks over to his dragon head

on his body and laughs. When they turn around, Lylock and Baron Milwr aren't looking at them as allies anymore. They are disgraced they could do such a thing. No honor. It was a test for Lylock. Either way, he was going to kill them. Lylock wanted to see for himself the untrustworthy race they have become.

"So I guess this means you are like Darron and Darryn, trading in your own king, eh?" Baron says.

Fyanicrum, Jupira, Derilyn, and Geulia haven't noticed that vines from the forest are about to grab them from behind. In an instant, the vines drag them back toward the curtain wall, pulling their bodies up the wall as they dangle in the air, swinging left to right like a vintage clock.

Mother Mary and Hynwyn look on with amazement. A lightning strike comes from the sky, shooting down like a comet smashing into the ground, with dirt and debris flying all over the place. It's Stratford. He has come to check on the progress of their raid on the castle.

Stratford made sure to wear his pink and yellow Emosiwn Melyn diamond coronet around his head. He wanted to say a few words to the last of the royal Cynforians.

"Did you really think we would keep you alive? You aren't House of Diablo Arches material. Both of you are too tall anyway," Stratford says, taunting the Cynfor dragons.

Without looking back, Stratford points to Baron Milwr to come closer. He looks toward the opening through the damaged Gates of Death, which leads down a narrow, mid-sized path of the destroyed Last Fairy Maze Forest.

Ceri, the fairy watcher, appears on one of the large trees that is slumped inside the main bailey.

"If it isn't the trustworthy fairy to come check up on us," Stratford says to Ceri.

"I have destroyed the curtain wall like you asked, master," she says.

Fyanicrum and Jupira are hanging upside down, knowing their lives are going to end before they know it.

"Baron, use your voice of destruction. Please end their miserable lives. They bore me," Stratford says, yawning with sarcasm.

194

Baron Milwr walks in front of Fyanicrum and Jupira, who are begging for their lives. He yanks the coronets from the heads of both of the traitors. Mary pulls the horse chess pieces from her back pocket, giving one of them to Hynwyn so they can hold them near their ears, for if they don't, they will die from Baron Milwr's life-killing voice.

Baron stands ready. Stratford walks up to Fyanicrum, Jupira, Derilyn, and Geulia, asking two questions before he lets Baron kill them.

"Where is the location of this world you have hidden from my senses? Where are Princess Nia and Tim? Tell me now!"

"You should have asked before you tricked us!" Fyanicrum says, spitting in Stratford's face. Knowing their lives are ending anyway, they refuse to talk as they dangle upside down on the curtain wall.

Stratford smacks the hell out of all of them then waves his hand toward Baron to end their lives immediately.

**"ROARRRRRRRR!!!!!!!!!!!!!!"**

Baron screams in a deadly octave, smashing their bodies against the stone wall like Welsh bread.

"Those traitors! Now it's up to you to find Princess Nia and Tim. I have bailed you out for the last time. You don't want to see yourselves like them, do you?" says Stratford, making death threats toward the House of Diablo Arches.

One of the Diablo Arches in command brings a scroll to Lylock, who immediately hands it to Stratford.

196

"Is this the scroll of Charun," says the commander.

Stratford looks down at the Welsh dactylic hexameter writing scroll, noticing the first wish has a line burnt through it, indicating it has already been used.

"Two wishes are left," Stratford whispers to himself. "This might come to some use when I have time to restore order in the Death of Ages."

He orders Lylock and Baron Milwr to head toward the outer regions to begin mining the Emosiwn Melyn diamonds once more. Stratford vanishes into thin air while the House of Diablo Arches head toward the outer regions, leaving only a few Diablo Arches to watch the grounds.

Mary and Hynwyn's plans have

now changed. The Death of Ages is now completely controlled by the House of Diablo Arches. Hynwyn knows there is only one way to end this tragedy.

"There are only a few more royal Houses in Selwyn's Chancer who have chosen to live in the outer regions of the Death of Ages. One of them is the *House of Vonixrians* who control the train of souls that arrive at the Gates of Death each year. We have to follow the tracks to their region," he says.

They run back up to the spiral staircase inside the spiral turret to get a few loose supplies, including Hynwyn's blade and battle axe. They sneak through all the abandoned hallways through the colosseum until they reach the outside of the castle where the River Styx and the Vonixrians' train tracks meet.

Mary tosses the chess pieces on the ground. In a flash, Jupiter's horses grow back to normal size. Mary and Hynwyn ride away without alarming the Diablo Arches, who remain at the castle.

"We will have to make it to the never-ending **Cliff of Wmfre.** We can summon a Trydan dragon to fly over the **Sky of Wymfreya** to the mountains of the fallen wizards from Windsor. This might be the only way they can defeat the Diablo Arches and save Princess Nia and Tim," Hynwyn says, knowing the newlyweds are unaware of what happened to her race.

Hynwyn Reese and Mother Mary ride to the far ends of the outer regions toward the *Cliff of Wmfre*. Mary worries for her only son.

As day turns into night, Hynwyn can hear howls from ancient wolves that thrive around the area.

"Not even the House of Vonixrians would go to the cliffs. They fear the wizards from Berkshire, England. They used to live under the Windsor Bridge before they were doomed to the Death of Ages for using their magic," Hynwyn says.

Jupiter's horses snort many times near some of the trees ahead of them. The horses move their heads from left to right, hearing birds chirp, sensing movement above in the trees as dawn moves quickly across the dark-blue horizon.

Light shines through the forest,

revealing a tall female figure sitting on a large branch in the trees above. Hynwyn, ready to defend himself and Mary, notices that the huge woman is Goddess Venus. She has come to inform them of what the future has in store for them, for they must be prepared to fight for their ultimate survival if they continue toward the never-ending *Cliff of Wmfre*.

# The Bluebells Forest

In a sacred and unknown part of the Death of Ages lies the Bluebells Forest with some of the most beautiful trees surrounding Cynfornia. The bluebell flowers sway in the breeze as Hyacinthoides non-scripta. They are bulbous perennial plants that make the forest seem like God took a little extra time to make them.

Cynfornia is perfect place to raise an heir of the House of Cynfor, in Princess Nia's mind. The white carriage rolls through the forest, down a parallel dirt road that leads to an abandoned castle built just for Princess Nia and her new husband, Tim Hartwell. When they birth a child, a magical army of Cynfornia will appear from behind a waterfall at the castle to protect the new kingdom of Cynfornia.

Tim looks around, falling in love with what he sees. Princess Nia holds Tim's hand. The white carriage breaks out of the forest into the circular driveway on the right-hand side of the castle. They can hear the waterfall behind the castle, which is filled with enough fish for them to eat forever. The forest surrounding them is filled with plenty of animals for them to hunt. The Bluebells Forest was built specifically for this moment. It has been abandoned for centuries, waiting for

Princess Nia, who never ages until she is married. Now that she has exchanged her vows, Princess Nia is finally be able to grow older with the love of her life. Her age will match Tim's, which is eleven-and-a-half-years old. She is happier than ever to be able to become a woman.

The carriage stops in front of the **Castle of Cynfornia**. The door opens, allowing Tim to step out. He turns around and holds his beautiful wife's hand. Her long bridal dress slides behind her as they look around, feeling the warmth from the sky above, listening to the birds sing in the warm fall wind.

At the end of next spring, Tim and Nia spend their 12th birthday together. Tim wants to give her a quick kiss on the cheek, so she wraps a lock of her hair behind her ear so Tim can kiss her sweet skin. His lips touch her cheek, which is as soft as can be. She wraps her arms around Tim, holding him tight, then proceeds up the steps to enter the *Castle of Cynfornia* for the very first time.

Walking up the steps, they notice how the steps are white marble with not one dirt stain on them, protected by the magic her grandfather, Miniver and Cynhafar, had blessed her with.

They continue up the steps as two lovely white doves fly right in front of them, making Nia smile from ear to ear. Her blonde hair is shining from the sun. Her blue eyes sparkle with every twist of her face. Somehow, music from a harp box is playing inside the castle, catching their attention. They run inside, noticing a stairwell that

205

leads up both sides of the large inner foyer. A fountain of water is in the middle of the foyer with a statue of Goddess Venus and her helpers in the center of the fountain. The helpers are holding vases that pour water into the fountain. The body of Goddess Venus lies in the center with the appearance of taking a bath, a true symbol of mythology right in front of them.

The melody is actually not coming from a harp box. Instead, the beautiful sound is coming from the large pink and yellow Emosiwn Melyn diamond chandelier above them, making the sweetest melodies of joy for them to hear.

"Cynfornia is more magical than I ever dreamed, my beautiful husband," Princess Nia says.

206

Tim leads them into the cloister garden where a large fire is burning for them to enjoy. The cloister has four corners overlooking the middle ward below them. The ward has private apartments with completely finished rooms in which they can raise their kids when the couple comes of age.

The private apartments are connected to a gateway that leads to the *White Tower*. A hoist leads all the way up the tower that's eleven meters shorter than the Elizabeth Tower in London, overlooking the horizon in the Death of Ages for as far as they can see. At this very moment, both Princess Nia and Tim Hartwell are worry-free about their young lives.

Night falls around the Bluebells Forest

as a large amount of altocumulus clouds cover the sky, leaving just enough light for the full moon to shine into the Royal Deanery.

Princess Nia and Tim enjoy their first meal in their new castle. Princess Nia is sitting right next to Tim so she can feel the warmth of his skin. She knows they can't have any intimacy, but she for sure wants to feel his warm body next to hers.

Tim cuts some of the deer meat from the fresh kill he brought from the forest. He used a bow and arrow from the weaponry ward on the first floor of the apartments. The bell in the Cynforian chapel is a replica of the bell in the *White Tower*. It rings eleven times, marking their age. After that, it will only ring once a year on their birthday.

Tim and Nia rush to their master bedroom. They notice the dishes have magically cleaned and packed themselves back into the cabinets in the kitchen area of the Royal Deanery. Tim and Princess Nia walk down the halls, laughing and giggling, then make their way back to their master bedroom private apartment. Both of them decide the castle is too big to explore tonight because of their long journey through the Bluebells Forest.

Once Tim opens the master bedroom, he notices the Shield of Aeneas leaning against the bed with the Book of Hartwell resting on top of his messenger bag on their bed. Linen drapes that dangle from a white canopy that covers their bed dance with the slight wind from the windows. Princess

Nia walks over to her personal closet filled with luxurious clothes. Each section is color-coded and includes fancy heels in different sizes for when she grows older. Princess Nia puts both of her hands on her face, for this is everything she could have dreamed of.

"Is all this for me?" Princess Nia whispers with joy. She is more excited than she has ever been. Luxurious jewelry begins to float inside her closet. All types of beautiful pendants, charms, necklaces, and rings in gold and silver float in front of her, including Cynforian Silhouette pieces that have been carved in the middle of some of them.

Tim is standing behind her while she enjoys every bit of her new life, including him. Princess Nia turns around and faces Tim, loving the life she has always dreamed of. The power of the *"Love of Venus"* has even forgiven Tim for what he has done to her father, Miniver and Cynhafar. They knew their sons, Bledri and Tomes, would never have kept their promise if the day had ever come.

Tim looks directly into her eyes, wiping her tears away. He kisses her on her cheek, then sits down, watching her try on some of the clothes before it gets too late. Her body begins swirling around as she tries on everything she possibly can.

Tim goes over to his closet and sees royal clothing that ranges from almost a thousand years ago to the present in British and Welsh culture. He is now a Prince of Cynfor, also the carrier of the magical Galon of Wales.

Midnight approaches and both of them jump into bed in their night clothes. A full moon is in perfect view from the window of their royal bedroom, and they look at it until they fall asleep.

Night flows into morning twilight. God's sunrays flow through the entire room. Tim wakes up, noticing that breakfast has magically appeared in their room: his favorite Welsh bacon, laver bread, hot tea, eggs, and crystal wine glasses filled with water and juice for them to drink.

"Good morning, honey. Should we visit the waterfall today?" Tim says.

Princess Nia is just getting up, putting slippers on her feet. She walks over to the breakfast table next to her husband and they smile at each other. They relax in the room and are not worried one bit. Princess Nia is excited for Tim to do exactly what he wants to do.

They walk across the walkway into the showers where natural-flowing water goes through the castle straight from the waterfall. They get ready and head outside to the waterfall to hear the sounds of nature and see what else this magical kingdom has to offer.

Where the Bluebells Forest connects to the waterfall, they notice the same white unicorn coming out of the forest, drinking some of the water, unafraid. Tim wraps his arm around Nia as they lie in the sun for hours. Tim brought a picnic basket from the castle, filled with fruits and vegetables for them to snack on. Princess Nia grabs some of the strawberries and feeds her husband. Then, the white unicorn comes right over to them, for it wants some of the sweet fruit and some of the lettuce to eat. Tim gives Nia some of the lettuce, and she holds it in her palm. The beautiful white unicorn steps back at first, then steps forward, eating from her hand.

Nia looks back at Tim with a golden smile as the unicorn begs for some of the fruit in the basket as well.

"I guess he is pretty hungry," Tim says.

Nia leans down and looks underneath the horse for a second. "It looks like it a girl from here," she says, laughing. The unicorn runs off, back into the Bluebells Forest.

"I wonder how the unicorn found us?" Tim says with curiosity.

214

"All living things in this forest can breathe the air, but that is the last magical unicorn on earth and in Selwyn's Chancer," Nia says.

Tim gets up and jumps into the cool water and begins to swim. Princess Nia jumps into the water after him as they wrestle a bit, having fun underneath the shining weather, with a single-cell cumulonimbus capillatus incus cloud in the sky.

The magical power of the Galon inside of Tim, and the *"Voice of Venus"* inside of Princess Nia, has made them wild for each other. Tim looks into her eyes, never wanting to see any other woman in his life. It's only the second day in Cynfornia, and both of them have almost completely forgotten about what they left behind.

Chapter 9: The Bluebells Forest

A few days pass, the sky goes from blue to orange while lightning strikes in the air. They were enjoying another day, relaxing at the waterfall. Rain begins to pour so they head back to the castle for the rest of the day. They dry off and head down to the library. There are shelves of books that reach to the ceiling, with a ladder to reach the highest ones.

Princess Nia picks out a few that she likes. Some of them are about becoming a mother and nursing children. Others are about a woman's responsibilities when she starts to ovulate.

Tim and Princess Nia sit side by side reading for a few hours near the fireplace. The sound of rain pouring on top of the castle is somewhat relaxing.

Tim looks over at Nia and puts his fingers through her hair. He holds her around the waist for he has never felt such love for someone. Tim is beginning to remember how his father left Tim's family at such an early age. In his heart he can feel that he wants to be the best father he can be. Princess Nia, still reading, stops and begins to speak.

"Do you love me, honey? I love you, more than life. I hope you always remember that."

Tim kisses her on her cheek and walks over to the fire, tossing on another log, even though he doesn't have to. He whispers his *Firewyn spell*, igniting the light-blue flame around his arms. Princess Nia looks at him with her eyes wide, wondering what he is doing.

"Humans able to control fire? Who would have ever thought." Tim says.

Princess Nia looks at him, staring at his arms, while Tim looks over to the fireplace.

"My love, let's make sure we keep things fresh while we're together," she says. "I never want you to feel that you don't want to be around me." Princess Nia reaches for his hands that are still on fire.

Tim quickly says *"Firewyn,"* extinguishing the fire wrapped around hands and wrist.

"Honey, you almost burnt yourself. Be careful," Tim says.

"I was just playing around. I knew you would put the flame out," she says as the day begins to wind down into late afternoon. For the rest of the night they play chess together then silently fall asleep.

For the next few months, Tim and Nia spend every morning and afternoon going outside, carving likenesses of each other out of marble. Both of them are trying the best they can, for Nia knows she can use her magic to straighten things out.

As more days go by leading into Halloween, they play trick or treat with each other and make candy together.

The night before Christmas while Nia is sleeping, Tim goes into the forest and plucks lots of pink roses, forming a bouquet for his lovely wife. When she wakes up Christmas morning he has many gifts wrapped for her. Together, they decorate the large Christmas tree in the library with all sorts of ornaments.

Princess Nia used her magic power to lift a huge pine tree from the forest, bringing it right into the library.

When they are ready to open each other's presents, Nia hands Tim his first one. Tim opens it and notices she has made a necklace for him with her picture engraved on the metal. The necklace has thirty three-carat Emosiwn Melyn diamonds going around it as well.

Tim is ready to show her the bouquet he designed for her in the shape of a heart. She looks at it and gets emotional. On this very day, they are happier than ever, spending their first Christmas together.

On New Year's, they sit in the *White Tower of the Cynfornia Castle*. Tim uses his *Firewyn spell* to shoot fireworks on the circular driveway. They look out the *White Tower* as fireworks go off for about an hour. They hold hands, watching the fireworks explode in all sorts of shapes in the sky over Cynfornia. For the very last one, Princess Nia waves her hand in the air, which makes the firework spell

"I love you" in the night sky.

On the first day of the new year, snow falls from the sky. Tim and Nia spend time together making snowmen and snow angels. Later that day, they notice the white unicorn coming out of the snow forest to play with them for a bit. They race around as the unicorn hangs around, then dashes off into the Bluebells Forest, covered in snow.

On Valentine's Day, Tim tries his best to make sure this is the best day his wife has ever had. When Princess Nia wakes up, she notices there are rose petals that lead out of the room, down the hallway, and through the gateway to the front of the castle. The rose petals direct her toward the right, leading her to the back of the castle facing the waterfall. Tim has set up a fire outside and a table that has hot cocoa and cookies for her to eat. He has also cut pieces of paper into a homemade letter.

"Go ahead, open it," Tim says.

Nia sits down with anticipation, not sure what's inside the letter. She opens it slowly and finds a poem written by Tim.

-----------------------------------------------------------------

Nia,
On this very day
I love you more than ever.

222

Forever I will stay by your side. Now Kiss me. Nia!

Your love.
TIM

------------------------------------------------------------

Nia jumps out of her seat, pouncing on Tim as he falls back into his chair. She uses her right hand to keep her hair from dangling in Tim's face. She gives Tim one of the longest sentimental kisses on the lips since they've been there.

Nia's love for Tim is growing. She knows their twelfth birthdays are coming up in April.

"Can you believe our birthdays are almost here? We will be twelve years old finally," she says.

223

Princess Nia begins to kiss Tim aggressively, knowing she is not supposed to, for she never kissed a boy until she got married. They both get up, knowing they must follow the order of marriage exactly as planned and not a day sooner.

They enjoy their hot cocoa and laver bread as they watch the waterfall flowing into the lake, which is frozen.

"Thank you for giving me such a wonderful first Valentine's Day," says Nia. "You don't even know how many times Fyanicrum and Jupira, or Derilyn and Guelia, tried to give me flowers and gifts on Valentine's Day, but I would never accept them. Those suitors weren't worthy of my love.

"Do you believe everything happens

for a reason?" she asks, for she is dying to know what he thinks about life and coincidences.

"I believe everything happens for a reason," Tim says. "I mean, I would have never dreamed of living a life in a magical land like Cynfornia, being married at eleven years of age to the most beautiful woman in the world. So the answer to your question? Yes, I believe everything happens for a reason.

"I have met some of the most legendary people in such a small time frame," Tim contines, "from Goddess Diana, Brutus of Troy, and Venus, but ..." Tim stops abruptly to tell her about something that has been bothering him.

"There is another girl from my school

225

back where I come from. She really liked me but now she is lost forever," he says.

Nia kisses him, putting her finger over his mouth. She knows it's hard for him.

The rest of the night they hold each other as they sit in front of the fireplace in the castle. She desperately wants to make things easy on him. Both of them are thinking about the next five years in Cynfornia.

During the night, Tim wakes up and hears voices from all the way down in the foyer in the front of the castle. He gets out of bed while Princess Nia is still asleep. Walking downstairs, he notices there is a large painting on the wall that wasn't there when they first arrived.

Tim looks at the painting, noticing it is of the Crystal Dynasty that Brutus of Troy mentioned during Tim's training. There are eight people in the oil painting in alphabetical order: Aeneas of Troy, Brutus' oldest sons; Albanactus, Locrinus, the first Roman emperor; Augustus, Brutus of Troy, the mighty Caesar of Rome; Emperor Claudius, Brutus' younger son; Kamber, and Paris of Troy.

Tim Hartwell looks at the picture, totally amazed, for it seems they were standing side by side while the painter illustrated their royal stances. Tim looks toward the bottom right-hand corner of the painting to see the name Federico Barocci signed in a golden ink.

"How can this be?" Tim ponders to himself, yawning from exhaustion. At this very moment, he knows the Goddesses

Venus and Diana have something to do with this. Not thinking anymore about it, he runs back upstairs to get more sleep and let destiny run its magical course.

Back on the other side of the Death of Ages, Hynwyn Reese and Mary are still standing in front of Goddess Venus. Both of them are wondering what she is about to say. Venus jumps down from the long tree branch above them. Due to her height, the ground rumbles a bit when she lands. She turns around; some of the deer that live in the forest can feel her presence.

Venus pets the fur on the side of one of the females. Mother Mary, more anxious than ever, wants to speak about why she is there. Before she can utter a few words,

Venus puts her hand in the air and points toward the moon.

When Hynwyn and Mary look up, they notice the moon getting closer and closer to them. The bright sphere passes through a cumulus arcus roll cloud. The moon's body pushes through the cloud, which leads into another set of cumulonimbus calvus clouds. Hynwyn and Mother Mary continue to look at the moon as it begins to take the shape of a woman who is illuminating through the trees. The glowing woman glides down the branches and lands right next to Venus. The moon has taken the shape of Goddess Diana. She is wearing a beautiful white dress, while Venus has a light-purple linen dress on. Both of them are wearing beautiful sheer scarfs and look like twins standing next to each other.

"Hello, you two. I see you are wanting to head toward the never-ending cliffs," Diana says. "There is a small problem with you wanting to travel there." Diana takes her left hand and removes the illumination from her body. She uses her fingers to throw magical dust into the air, which travels through the branches and rises into the sky. As the dust goes through the cumulonimbus calvus cloud, a large lightning bolt bursts through its mist. The magical dust continues to head upward in the atmosphere and takes the shape of a ring. The ring begins to fill itself until it is full and looks like a crescent moon.

Hynwyn and Mother Mary look on, waiting for them to speak their peace.

230

Goddess Venus and Diana hold each other's hands and transport the four of them to the Bluebells Forest in Cynfornia, for there is something Hynwyn and Mary must see.

Their bodies transport to the circular driveway at the Castle of Cynfornia. Hynwyn and Mary look around at this magical world. Mary notices the air smells a bit different from air in the Death of Ages. A million times fresher.

"I'm not going to take you inside and disturb what must be. I have brought you here to show you that this is the future. Without Cynfornia, there will be no future for the people in Selwyn's Chancer. I wanted to show you that I helped Tim get here, Mary, as I got my son Aeneas to Rome. Imagine if he had never reached Latium. Where would the world be then?" Diana says.

"I don't think anyone on earth can even muster an answer," Mother Mary replies. "I thank you for helping my son, but do you think it was right for you to interfere with Princess Nia and have her fall in love with him?"

Venus looks at them and taps Goddess Diana on the shoulder, for no human has ever been bold enough to judge her motives.

Goddess Diana claps her hands, sending them to the land of Llyn Cwellyn just before midnight. They look at the reservoir moving below them. As the moon reaches between Mynydd Mawr and Snowdon, Charun flows his boat into the water. He rides up to them at a slow pace. Venus looks at Charun and tosses him five ancient coins with Caesar's face on them. Charun, sticking his hand out, tosses the coins into his lower deck. He then turns around and points toward the castle to the House of Scorpus behind him.

"We aren't going there. I just wanted to show you the world Brutus of Troy found when he traveled to these lands. There are many parallel worlds on Earth. Some have been found, some have not."

"Hold on. Didn't Stratford make Selwyn's Chancer?" Hynwyn says.

"Yes, of course, but little did he know Brutus of Troy would find a royal House of Scorpus who have the capability to reach the Death of Ages. I hope you see the chain of events unfolding in Selwyn's Chancer. For

233

your son, Tim, must not escape the Death of Ages as of yet," Diana says.

"What about our family's Book of Hartwell? I am sure Stratford has something up his sleeve to stop him from getting out," Mother Mary says, brushing her hair into a ponytail with her hands.

"That was before Tim married Princess Nia. Now there is a new prophecy he will have to defend or the reality worlds in which you live in Tenby will be no more. Stratford's ultimate goal is to merge both worlds and make Earth his world," Venus says as the planet Jupiter flies into the sky, slowing down near the moon. Venus points to Mercury arriving around the same time.

"Something is up. The planets are listening. The universe is wanting to know exactly what is going on on Mother Earth. We must leave now!" Diana and Venus say in unison, sending Mary and Hynwyn back to the Death of Ages' outer region. Venus and Diana have helped them by transporting them to the *Cliff of Wmfre*. Mary and Hynwyn are astonished by the cloud formations ahead of them. Cirrus floccus, cirrus radiatus, cirrus spissatus undulatus, cirrocumulus stratiformis, and cirrus fibratus radiatus clouds are everywhere.

Hynwyn points toward altocumulus lenticularis duplicatus clouds that are far away from the cliff.

"This must be the *Sky of Wymfreya* over there. The Wizards of Windsor live there," says Hynwyn, who uses his human hand to pull out a Scorpus conical horn to summon a Trydan dragon to fly there. The horn is so small that he implanted it in his claw. No one knew he ever had it on him at the castle of the House of Scorpus.

"Are you ready to fly?" Hynwyn asks, blowing the horn with its distinct sound.

"Only the lungs of a Scorpus scorpion can blow this instrument," he says as they look above, noticing the clouds are moving, pushing together like cotton candy. Hynwyn informs Mary that this particular Trydan doesn't stop moving. When the wing gets close to the edge of the cliff, they will have to jump for it.

The head of the Trydan dragon makes a fallstreak hole in the altocumulus stratiformis translucidus lacunosus cloud above. Gliding down toward the cliff,

236

Hynwyn and Mother Mary hold hands, jumping off the *Cliff of Wmfre* into the depths of the stratocumulus castellanus cumulogenitus cloud. They can't see a thing as they glide over the *Cliff of Wmfre*. Only with hope from the gusts of wind shall they make a safe landing on the wings of an ancient Trydan dragon.

Y Diwedd
(The End)

237

Coat of Arms

# Coat of Cynfor

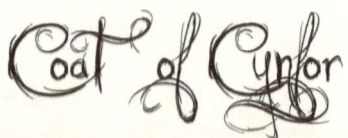

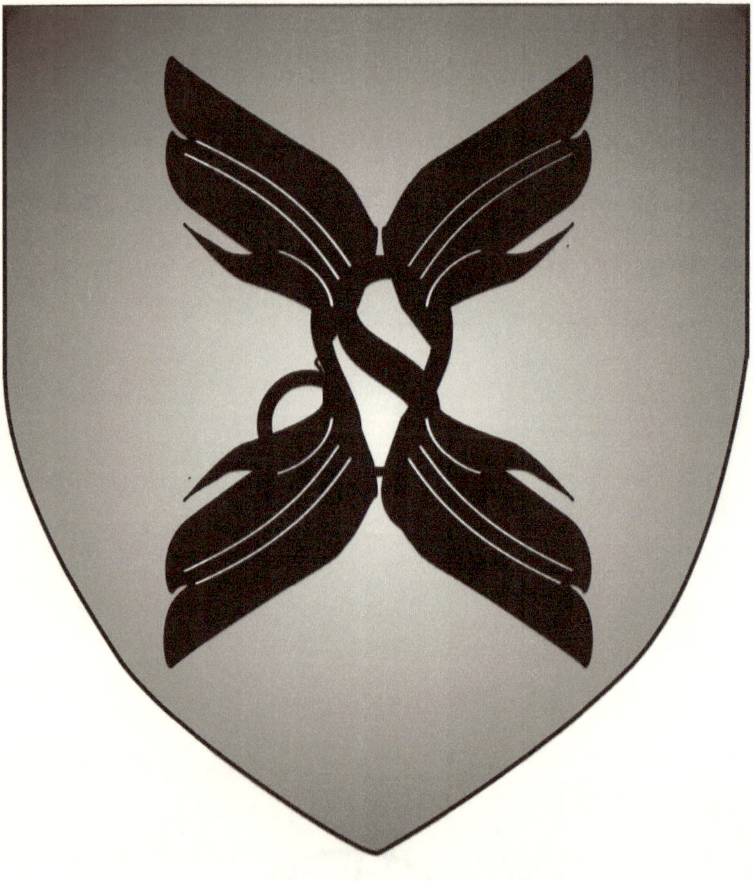

(Worn by The House of Cynfor)

**Senate Hall**

Rank below 3rd to Throne

TIM HARTWELL and The Death of Ages

(Worn by The House of Cynfor)
**Gatekeepers**
Personal Guard
*[Protectors of Throne/Gates of Death]*
239

# Coat of Cynfor

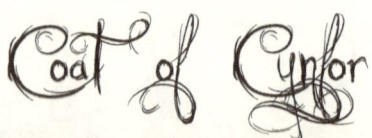

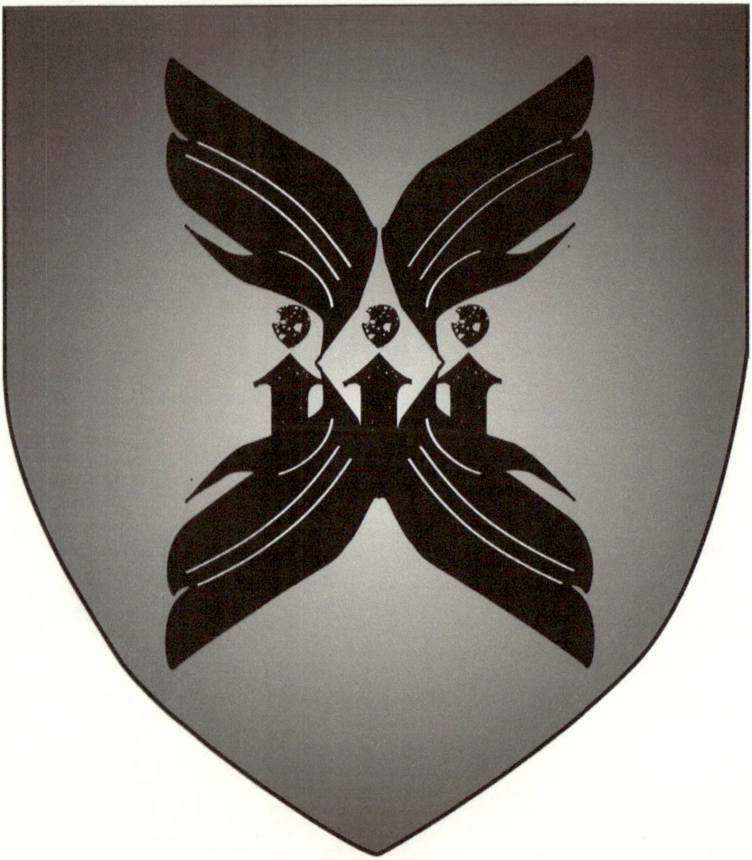

(Worn by The House of Cynfor)

**Fyanicrum/Jupira & Derilyn/Geulia**

3rd to Throne

*[Sons of Bledri & Tomes]*

TIM HARTWELL and The Death of Ages

(Worn by The House of Cynfor)
**Bledri & Tomes**
Rulers to the Throne
*[Sons of Miniver & Cynhafar]*

241

# House of Cynfor
## Death of Ages

UNDER THE EARTH OF MOUNTAIN MYNYDD MAWR LIES THE DEATH OF AGES. THE NEW RULERS TO THE HOUSE OF CYNFOR, BLEDRI AND TOMES, CONTROL THE MINES TO THE MOST PRECIOUS MINERAL IN STRATFORD'S SELWYN'S CHANCER, PARALLEL WORLD TO WALES. THE PINK & YELLOW EMOSIWN MELYN DIAMONDS WERE PREVIOUSLY CONTROLLED BY THE RUTHLESS HOUSE OF DIABLO ARCHES.

# Death of Ages

LOCATION: UNDERNEATH SNOWDON
NANT Y BETWS, GWYNEDD, NORTH WALES

ENTRANCE

# Bluebells Forest

LOCATION: UNKNOWN REGION
DEATH OF AGES, SELWYN'S CHANCER

Exit to Cynfornia

# Bluebells Forest

LOCATION: UNKNOWN REGION
DEATH OF AGES, SELWYN'S CHANCER

# Castle of Cynfornia

ONLY PRINCESS NIA & HER NEWLYWED WIZARD HUSBAND TIM HARTWELL, HAVE THE MAGICAL ABILITY TO BREATHE THE AIR IN THE BLUEBELLS FOREST. THIS PLACE IS SPECIAL FOR THE MARRIED COUPLE WILL SPEND THE NEXT FIVE YEARS THERE, UNTIL NIA BEARS AN HEIR TO THE HOUSE OF CYNFOR.

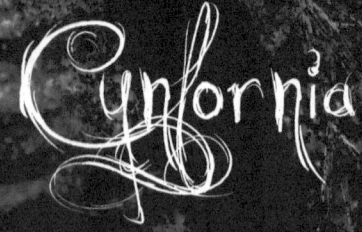

Cynfornia

LOCATION: UNKNOWN REGION
DEATH OF AGES, SELWYN'S CHANCER

# Death of Ages

is the lower region of Selwyn's

Chancer, the parallel world to Wales.

Created by a man named Strafford,

the Death of Ages where dead

spirits are transported by Charun

except for some paying spirits sent

by the House of Scorpus.

247

Hen Wlad Fy Nhadau

(Welsh: Land of My Fathers)